THE CANING

THE LASH HEARD AROUND THE WORLD

B.B. Wilkerson

ISBN 978-1-957943-19-0 (paperback)
ISBN 978-1-957943-20-6 (hardcover)
ISBN 978-1-957943-21-3 (digital)

Rushmore Press LLC
1 800 460 9188
www.rushmorepress.com

Printed in the United States of America

Preface

Authors are often asked why they write what they write, especially when there appears to be an agenda behind the fiction. I will freely admit that my aim is to focus on some events that may have been forgotten but need attention in the age of terrorism.

The fictionalized story is based on an event in history, and many details are lifted from journalistic accounts. News reports and prominent persons are sometimes quoted verbatim, while others are imagined. I changed the names of many of those involved and apologize if any of those named are actual persons, as I never met any of them, and I was not present at the time. I can definitely say that the lead character's actions, thoughts, and words in this novel are fabricated and not meant to imply anything other than that he was caned unjustly.

Of course, a more historical account, with footnotes, could have been written. One book that influenced me is *The Singapore Puzzle*, which was written by a group of academics, a journalist, and a former member of the government. Many newspaper accounts also helped the construction of events. To ensure that the account is fictionalized, I invent the country of Singland.

Yet careful scholarly reconstructions of events often miss the emotional essence of what occurred. In Machiavelli's vocabulary, the government was feared but not loved. The term Clobbering Machine, used by some foreigners to refer to the government, is an accurate portrayal of the totalitarian way in which the leaders then operated.

Readers will wonder why I have chosen to fabricate a sexual element in the re-telling of events. I don't remember exactly when, but the gay-oriented website *www.trevvy.com* emerged sometime during the first decade of the twenty-first century, displaying photos of extraordinarily muscular men from Asia. Much later came *Fifty Shades of Gray*, the best-selling novel about a woman who agreed to be a man's sex slave. American prisons are rumored notoriously to allow sex between prisoners, in which stronger men subjugate weaker men. Even rape of men in the U.S. military has been reported.

Accordingly, I realized that I had a hook for a novel: Convert some events to chapters, add sex as an element, and the result would be riveting reading—something that a reader could not put down after starting. What began as a short story soon became a full-length novel, but I didn't want to pad the narrative lest the reader would be bored.

There is also a racist element in the story, with the main American character as "whiteboy." At one point, he is even called "Jewboy." There are several reasons for inserting such a controversial element into the story. First, the Asian values movement in the early 1980s, contrasted a community-oriented Asia with an individualistic West as if the two were alternative choices. But the real feeling behind the movement was the belief that Asian Values are superior to Western values, and exact quotations in the story herein clearly demonstrate that thesis. A second reason for playing up that element is the fact that some Chinese actually believe in their superiority, even today. The unilateral assertions of power by the People's Republic of China in recent years are consistent with the view that China can set its own rules for the international community, which in turn must follow them. Similarly, the standards of justice are held to be self-evidently superior to those in the West. Claims that harsh punishment deters crime have never been verified with statistical proof. In fact, the number of canings per year has been about the same over the years, suggesting the opposite.

I focus on caning herein because that form of corporal punishment, a clear violation of the International Covenant on Civil and Political Rights, continues unabated in some countries today—in homes, in government and private schools, as well as in prisons. The symbolism of caning is that those who are treated in such a manner are considered as children or even as animals, not fully human beings. That such a barbaric form of punishment would continue officially in the twenty-first century is a function of a ruthless ruling class in the island republic. What is baffling is that Britain originally introduced caning into its former colonies, treating colonial subjects as children. Caning has no connection whatever with the historic values of Buddhism and Confucianism that leaders have presumed to be the foundation for the Asian Values thesis. If this book creates a movement to ban caning, then the purpose of the novel will be well served.

However, caning is only part of the story. Police torture is also an element. The pattern of arrest followed by torture to produce a confession seems out of step with a world in which human rights were vastly improving around the world after the end of the Cold War. But 9/11 changed that. The United States foolishly adopted torture as a counterterrorism strategy, and the result has been an increase in terrorism. I draw a straight line between the experiences described herein to the policies adopted in Washington after 9/11.

Lastly, many readers may wonder whether the author has written other works of fiction. The answer is no. Indeed, I have chosen a pseudonym that cannot be googled. (My first name is not "Bob" or "Bryan" because I do not use a first name, only initials.) I prefer to let the present work of fiction stand on its own rather than trying to promote acceptance by citing major accomplishments of my career in an entirely different area of human activity. Instead, I leave the ultimate judgment over what I have written to you, the reader.

B. B. Wilkerson

Introduction

I have an important story to tell. Actually, a confession. There was a time in my life when I was caught up in a drama that nobody should have to experience. As a teenager, I was ignorant of many things. I first had to learn how Chinese adjust to life in a dictatorship. I discovered the hard way what can happen when you are a pawn in the wrangling of international politics. I was transformed overnight from a decent but somewhat wild teenager to a helpless boy in prison. I discovered behind bars that I had to do the bidding of someone very handsome and muscular or experience sexual degradation. I thus found myself submitting to Chinese discipline for survival in a prison that still haunts my nightmares. Then the real punishment came. Strikes of the cane on my butt by a kungfu master are responsible for permanent marks on my body today, thirty years later.

My odyssey began during summer break in 1993. During the month of July, I visited my father and his lovely new Chinese bride in Singland. I was immediately enchanted by the country's tropical paradise. With my father and stepmother, I toured the country and some lovely areas in the surrounding countries. During that short trip, I met a breathtakingly cute and beautiful girl named Ling who went to the airport to say farewell when I flew home to the United States at the end of my vacation trip.

Soon after I returned home to a suburb of Philadelphia, I asked Mom an important question. Instead of continuing my senior year at a boarding school in Massachusetts, I wanted to finish my high school education in Singland before going to college back in the USA. After warning me of the dangers of life in a dictatorship, she agreed. Off I went to Singland in late August, just before the new school term started.

Here's my story.

1

Arrival

As the airplane edged close to the city that day in mid-August, I was wowed again by the scene of lights from tall buildings reflecting on the water. A picture postcard. I never imagined that Singland would shine so beautifully at night from the air. I had said goodbye to Mom many hours ago in Philly, and I was looking forward to having Dad greet me at the airport with his new curvaceous Chinese bride. Clearing customs at the airport was a breeze. I collected my suitcases, tucked my light blue muscleshirt into my faded jeans, and exited into the secure area.

"Welcome again to Singland, Jimmy!" my father Donald said enthusiastically, with a big smile.

He was wearing a white polo shirt and blue pants that I remember he was wearing when we lived together in Pennsylvania. I guess he was trying to make me feel at home.

"You are now back in paradise, Jimmy!" my stepmother Yan Freeman chimed in, hugging and kissing me, wearing a shiny Chinese-patterned silk dress.

They were quite a pair: His 5'10" gaunt body towered over Yan's 5'5".

"How was the trip, Jimmy?" Dad asked.

"The 2- hour layover in Chicago sucked, Dad, but I fell asleep by the time we were over the Pacific," I said sleepily. "The food was pretty good, but I missed chocolate for dessert."

It was just after midnight. We stepped out onto the curb and entered a Cadillac limousine, with a driver named Corky Rahman waiting to take us from the airport to their apartment on Keppel Bay Drive, overlooking the water.

As I surveyed the magical-appearing lights from the ground while our elderly Malay driver sped up the East Coast Parkway, the car radio blasted news:

"Today, the temperature is expected to reach 95 degrees, relative humidity 81 percent. In local news, a thief received 12 strokes of the cane today for his part in a holdup at Lucky Plaza . . ."

"The cane?" I asked. "They do that here?"

"Only for serious crimes," Dad assured. "It's a deterrent. There's very little crime here, Jimmy." (He then bought government propaganda about a city free of crime.)

We passed six men wearing neon-green uniforms with the words "CORRECTIVE WORK ORDER" on their vests, cleaning a park.

"See those men," Yan pointed out. "They were litterbugs. That's how the government deals with littering, Jimmy."

"If you have even a small amount of marijuana," Dad confided, "they throw the book at you. You could even get the death penalty."

"And get rid of any chewing gum you brought," Yan warned. "If you give chewing gum to your school chums, you could go to jail for a year and pay a $14,000 fine."

"A business executive recently forgot to flush the toilet in a shopping mall," Dad added, "but cameras spotted him, and the police arrived before he left the toilet. Not only did he pay a $200 fine but his picture was prominently displayed on the front page of the local newspaper as a lawbreaker."

"Wow! They're really strict here," I then said, with a comical tone. "This must be a *fine* city!"

We all laughed.

Arriving at the apartment building, we were greeted by the colorful Gurkha doorman, dressed like some sort of Vatican guard, who remembered me from the past July, and said, "Hi! Fighting the Z-Monster?" (Gurkhas are members of the warrior class in Nepal, often deployed by the British to perform feats similar to American Marines.)

"I'm doing my best, Noroth."

I must have looked very tired. ("Z-Monster" is a Singlish term used when someone is so sleepy that he can hardly stay awake. The local creole language, Singlish, is a combination of English, various Chinese dialects, and Malay.)

> "See that camera, Jimmy?" Yan said, pointing to the outside of the condo. "It's there to catch litterbugs."

While the driver drove off, we entered the building by thumbprint rather than key, went into the elevator after three middle-aged male passengers, smelling of alcohol, exited. It was Saturday night.

Dad pushed floor 30, and the elevator rose smoothly to the penthouse floor in a few seconds.

> "The elevator also has a detector, Jimmy," Dad explained during the ascent. "If you urinate, it locks you in, and the alarm sounds."

> "Cool! Let's get to the top fast or I'll set off the sound!"

We laughed again.

We exited from the elevator to the penthouse. There was a sweeping view of night lights as soon as we entered. After we took off our shoes, as is the custom, I headed right for the hall bathroom.

The penthouse was very modern. Two bedrooms, a large living room with a 180° view enclosed in glass, a kitchen with red tile on the counters, a study with two desks, and several stacked bookshelves. Two very sleek bathrooms with glass-enclosed showers. White floor tile throughout, with modernistic throw rugs and runners. The furnishings were very sleek, including abstract paintings on the walls.

When I came into the living roo m, Yan asked,

"Hungry, Jimmy?"

"No, ma'am, I just wanna catch up on my sleep."

"Here's your pad again, Jimmy," Dad said proudly, opening the door to my room.

"Awesome!" I exclaimed.

My room overlooked the glittering harbor, though I didn't spot any ships. After taking my suitcases into the room, I picked up the phone near the desk and dialed up Newton Square, Philadelphia.

"Hello," Mom answered.

"I made it, Mom! The flight was smooth but too long and a little boring. But I'm here at last."

"I'm glad you're safe. What do you plan tomorrow, son?"

"I don't know. Right now, I'm gonna crash. I'm totally pooped."

"OK. Good night. Have a good time. I love you, Jimmy."

"Thank you, Mom. I love you, too."

I crawled into bed next to empty bookshelves and slept soundly until the light of the morning awakened my eyes, which had been almost bleary when I hit the sheets.

Dad was a corporate executive who'd been commuting to Singland, off and on, for the past three years. He didn't tell me that he found a beautiful bride until after the divorce. Mom got my sister Penny and the house in suburban Newton Square, just outside Philadelphia. Dad got me in the divorce, but I was at boarding school. He was transferred to the city of his dreams to start a new life with the most gorgeous woman I've ever seen. I agreed to join Dad for the adventure of living in a new culture.

I was still in high school, and I was eager to show off my athletic prowess and meet Ling again. I dreamed all night about taking her out on the town the following weekend.

2

Sunday

When I woke up at 9, I smelled bacon, eggs, rice, and soy sauce. I peeped out from my room and found Yan fixing breakfast. I quickly put on my robe and popped out, hair disheveled and all.

"May I join you for breakfast?" I asked kindly.

Yan responded, "Of course, Jimmy!"

Dad, at the dinner table already eating toast and jam alongside a plate of scrambled eggs, bacon, and rice, added,

"Join the party, Jimmy!"

I then unpacked a bit and showered. While looking at Keppel Bay through the window of our penthouse, I put on my tee-shirt emblazoned "Philadelphia" and my freshly purchased jeans and sandals. After leaving my room, I sat at the dinner table and quickly devoured it all. Dad was on the lazy boy, reading the *Straits Times*. My stepmother Yan sure knew how to please my tastebuds!

After the meal, while Yan was clearing plates from the table and washing the dishes, I stared at the scene in the harbor, where boats were moving past us.

> Dad said, "Today, Jimmy, we're picking up Ling about noon and taking you around the island so you can get familiar with where everything is. If that's OK with you."

> "Great!" My heart leaped for joy. I went to my room and got out my new tennis shoes, ready for the ride.

While still in my room, I called Ling.

> "Hey, Ling, I'm back. My family says we'll pick you up around 12 so we can go around the island together?"

> "Yes, they told me last week, Jimmy. I'm so happy to see you again, lah," Ling answered.

(In Singlish, "lah" is used to emphasize what the sentence has said.)

> "And I'm *so* eager to be with *you* again, Ling. Where we go is less important."

> "Me, too, Jimmy. We have a lot to catch up on, lah."

I didn't know what she meant at the time, but within a week, I learned that she was being pursued by someone else.

> "See you soon!" I was very upbeat, hoping to charm her. "I'll be out in front at noon, waiting for you all, lah." I wore a big smile as I put down the phone.

When everyone was ready, we went down the elevator and past our doorman, Pandita Rai, who tipped his hat. Musa Osman, a Malay limousine driver, came up, and all three of us got in. I was in the back seat. He drove us to Ling's apartment in Queenstown, going left and right through a maze of streets.

When we arrived, Ling was waiting in a beautiful light blue blouse with matching slacks. I got out of the car to greet her, and we lightly kissed and hugged. Then I opened the car door for her, she got in, and I joined her in the back of the limo. She was 5'6" and had a nice body. What attracted me to her was that she smiled a lot, and I liked the way she talked in a friendly tone.

"How have you been, Ling?" I asked, smiling.

Ling beamed, "I've had a wonderful summer, Jimmy, and I really look forward to joining you at the International School this year, lah. Will you go out for sports?"

"Yes, basketball and maybe football, Ling. I gotta keep myself fit!" I said proudly, showing my right bicep.

Dad interjected, "You know, Jimmy, that here football is soccer."

"Yes, Dad," I voiced, indicating that I knew that all along.

Ling chimed in, "And Jimmy will be the star of the teams, lah!"

Yan added, "Of course. Jimmy will be America's best contribution to local sports."

I grinned, though I really didn't need any flattery.

That day, we saw almost all points of interest in the island. The design is totally awesome! Many parks with beautiful flowers. We started at the Botanic Gardens, near Ling's apartment. Then we went west, stopping at the Chinese and Japanese gardens and the Science Center in Jurong. Next, up north to the nature preserve at Bukit Timah and the Orchid Garden, across the island to Changi Village and the Changi Murals. Then along the East Coast Park toward the Central Business District, the colonial-style buildings including Raffles Hotel, Parliament, past Canning Park, and along the hotels of Orchard Road. The limo went south to Chinatown and past our condo building to Mount Faber, and we boarded the cable car to Sentosa Island, where we saw golden-tanned swimmers. The roads were clean and modern, bordered by lush vegetation.

After returning from Mount Faber on the cable car, we went to the campus of Singland University and then Musa drove to a posh restaurant in Clementi.

As we got out of the limo in front of the restaurant, I exclaimed,

> "So beautiful! I just love Singland!"

> Ling said, "I'm so glad you like our little country, Jimmy."

> "It's not really little, Ling. There's a lot here!"

Dad, seemingly correcting me,

> "Actually, Singland is five times larger than Philadelphia. It's much, much bigger than Manhattan. Almost half the size of Long Island. But

the people are much more polite and keep the island
gleamingly clean."

Yan, supporting him,

> "I was born in Taiwan, but Singland has a lot more
> to offer."

We sat down to a delicious but spicy Chinese meal at Soup Restaurant
in Clementi Mall—very shiok (tasty). I tried to use chopsticks but
failed. Ling then put her hand on mine to guide my fingers on how
to pick up prawns. (That's what they call shrimp in Singland.)

We chatted over the meal. Small talk, but I got to sit next to Ling in
the circular table with a lazy-susan in the interior. I put my hand on
her right leg under the table. She smiled modestly as if I shouldn't be
too forward with her in public.

After the meal, we returned to the limo and Musa headed back to
Ling's apartment.

> "Tomorrow," Dad announced, "I'm taking Jimmy
> to the International School early to register and then
> join classes on the first day of school."

> "Boy, I'm looking forward to that!"

Then Ling cautioned,

> "Be careful at school about our friendship, Jimmy.
> Don't let everyone know immediately, as some
> Chinese guys are always trying to carry my books."

> "Huh?" I said, puzzled. "What do you mean, Ling?"

Ling explained,

> "Some Chinese guys think they own the island and the girls in it. Three-fourths here are Chinese. Jimmy, we can meet outside the school with no problem, but there might be some jealous Chinese guys, especially the athletes, so you don't want to start out too boldly. Get accepted first, Jimmy. Then we can pretend that we first met at school and carry on more easily."

Like yesterday, I intoned,

> "Whatever! Singland's a *fine* city!"

We all laughed.

Then the limo stopped at Ling's apartment in Queenstown. I went around the car to open the door for her. As she got out, she said,

> "I hope to see you tomorrow, lah."

With a smile, a hug, and a kiss, I responded,

> "You bet! For sure! *Secretly!*"

We laughed, and she went to the door of her apartment. We waved at each other, and I got back in the limo. I felt I had met the love of my life.

As we returned to our condo, my stepmom Yan intervened,

> "Foreigners aren't immediately accepted here. I know, Jimmy. When I came from Taiwan, I had problems at first. Thank goodness I met your Dad."

"Well," I said, "I came to Singland for a challenge. And I'll do my best! I'll show the guys who's the best athlete!"

Dad, "Don't get too cocky, Jimmy. The local guys are good at kung fu. You may have to learn that, too."

I said, "When the time comes, Dad, I'll master kung fu, too!" I probably sounded too punky, but I didn't want anyone to discourage me.

When we got back to our penthouse, I thanked Dad.

"What a perfect day! Singland is really cool, Dad!"

I showered, watched TV news and sports a little, and then went to sleep about the same time as my parents. I was looking forward to meeting the kids at school and joining the basketball and football (I mean soccer) teams.

3

Monday, School Day

After breakfast, Dad declared,

"This morning, Jimmy. I'm taking you to the International School. It places students at the best universities around the world."

"Dad, do their sports teams ever win competitions?" I asked hopefully.

"Yes, Jimmy" he assured. Unlike yesterday's cautious note, he said, "And with you, they'll win even more!"

Yan added while working on an abstract oil painting,

"You'll like the school, Jimmy. There're students from many countries, mostly Asia."

"Cool. I wanna learn about Asian cultures, especially Chinese."

We left the condo, going past the same doorman, who tipped his hat. Another Malay limousine driver, Jed Hisyam, came up, and both of us boarded. We headed for the International School on Preston Road between two green parks. I got out of the car and said "Goodbye!" to Dad who then went to work at the World Trade Center near our condo.

As I entered the school at 8, I saw a room for registration. After registration, which was very formal (passport for name, address, previous schooling, etc.), I was directed to the main auditorium, where at 9, the headmaster, Lee Sang Yim, presided over an assembly. He was a mousy little man with glasses. Not a leader by any means, he was short and thin, and spoke timidly:

"Welcome to ISS—International School Singland."

The students applauded.

"Will all the new students stand up?"

I rose from my chair along with about 120 others, mostly Chinese, and the rest clapped to greet us.

The headmaster motioned us to sit and continued,

> "We were founded in 1981 by Chan Chee Seng.
> The school enrolls 750 students aged 4 to 18, from
> kindergarten to grade 12. Here, at the high school,
> we have the most—400 students."

He didn't mention that a fourth of the students live with guardians, as their parents live outside Singland.

> "We are very selective about admission, and we turn
> away about 900 applicants each year. Our teachers
> expect the best from all students." Turning to the
> teachers in the front row, "Teachers, stand up!"

About 35 men and women stood up in the front and faced the rest of us. Applause again.

> "Some 50 different nationalities are represented from around the world, boys and girls of all races. It is our aim to provide a multicultural educational environment so that our students will achieve academic success, personal growth, and become socially responsible and active global citizens with an appreciation of learning as a life-long process. We strive to make a difference in the lives of our students."

Someone at the back, who had been the first to applaud, started to clap again, and everyone joined in. But I figured that he was a plant, and students were applauding because they felt somehow obligated.

> "We are accredited by the Western Association of Schools and Colleges in California. You can be sure that when you graduate, you will be accepted into the best schools in Australia, Britain, Canada, or the United States."

Applause again.

> "The athletic team is called the Mustangs, and we almost always defeat our rivals in sports."

A cheer came from the audience, "We are the Mustangs! We always win!"

I didn't see any Ford Mustangs anywhere in town! Or any horses for that matter. I wondered why they had such a Western cowboy name.

Apparently disapproving the outburst, Lee continued,

"Those in Grades 11 and 12 are required, before graduation, to participate in the Creativity, Action, and Service program. You must complete at least 150 hours of extracurricular activities outside school this year."

"Among the extracurricular activities are the Chess Club, Model United Nations, Language Clubs, Stock Market Club, Environmental Club, and many others. Artsy students can choose from Hip Hop dancing, Art Club, music and drama productions, and Newspaper Club. Last year, we produced the musical *Oklahoma*, and it was a great success, attracting attendance from around the island."

I heard a moan from some boys. I agreed. That stuff was not for me.

The headmaster went on,

"Students train for and compete in interschool sports. We offer badminton, basketball, cross country track, gymnastics, kung fu, netball, soccer, and swimming."

("Netball" was their word for volleyball.)

He didn't mention that Middle School students were expected to choose from basketball, gymnastics, soccer, tae kwon do, volleyball, and yoga. It was in gymnastics, I discovered later, where they got their start at building muscles.

After his boring but very short speech, Lee dismissed us to go to our classes, which were pre-assigned. During each class, I was introduced as a new student and applauded by the rest. My first course was history. Then math, followed by English, and beginning Mandarin Chinese. After lunch came chemistry. The last class was Gym.

4

First Classes

As I entered the first classroom, there was a map on the sidewalls, a blackboard in front, and posters in the back. When the teacher, Mr. Ching, arrived, all students, mostly Asian, stood up.

> Mr. Ching: "You may be seated, students . . . I want to recognize a new student in the class, James Freeman. He comes from America, but we won't hold that against him, will we?"

While applauding, Asian students smiled smugly. But Caucasian students looked peeved. Students were about half guys and half girls, as in most classes.

While passing out the textbook, Mr. Ching said,

> "We'll begin our history class with ancient China, the Xia Dynasty of about 4,000 years ago. Be sure to do the reading in Chapters 1 and 2 and be prepared to answer questions. Tomorrow, we will discuss Asian traditions and values, the main reason why Asia's on the rise and the West's on the decline."

I never experienced racism before. Now, on the first day of class, I sort of sensed I was already a victim of a racial slur. But I tried to forget about it, though it still bothered me. Better not get too emotional, I said to myself philosophically: "You're in a new country, and you should expect different and even strange things."

Because the assembly took away time from the first class, we were dismissed early.

I then went to math class, where Mrs. Tan explained the rudiments of geometry after greeting me as the newest student. Alistair McEwen, also in the class, winked as I entered. I would see him later at lunch.

After that came English. After I was introduced, Mrs. Lee had us take turns reading the first chapter of *Great Expectations* aloud.

> She explained the interesting background of "It was the best of times. It was the worst of times," and asked us "Which times were we now living in?"
>
> Some Chinese students said "Worst." Many non-Chinese said "Best."
>
> But some said "good and bad times today."

We were assigned to read the next five chapters and report our insights during the next class.

The Chinese Mandarin class, the most difficult for me, consisted of mostly non-Chinese students. The teacher, Mrs. Wen, told us that we would learn the basic characters and the Mandarin dialect, which wasn't commonly used in Singland. Most local Chinese spoke Hakka. Mandarin was the preferred dialect at school, I guess, due to its association with the upper classes in China.

5

Lunch

During lunch, we filed into the cafeteria. The food offered was a mixture of cuisines—American, Chinese, European, and Indian. We could choose between soft drinks and tea. A tiny dessert was offered—usually an Asian delicacy.

After filling my tray with food, I looked around the room for somewhere to sit. The room had picnic-type benches allowing about six per table. Not immediately seeing Ling, I decided to sit with four Caucasian boys and a black guy who were already seated.

> "Hi," I said, as I sat down. "My name's Jimmy. I'm from Philadelphia. My dad works at the World Trade Center here." The others introduced themselves.

> "I'm Eduardo from Chicago. My mom works at the American Embassy. Mucho gusto!" At 5'11", he seemed very athletic and friendly.

> "My name is Alistair. My parents are at the British Council. I saw you at math class." Almost as tall as me, he appeared book-oriented.

"Jean-Marc," he said with a French accent and some food in his mouth.

He was a black guy, about 5'7", not athletic. Probably his parents were from one of the former African colonies, I mused.

"My parents are at the French embassy in Sri Lanka, but they thought this was the best place in the region for me to go to school. I live in the dorm."

"Call me Charlie," said the last guy with almost an American accent. "I'm racially mixed, part Irish and part Chinese, living here with my parents. My dad runs the Hyatt Hotel. My mom is at the Canadian embassy. I'm also new. The government moves my mom from country to country every three years."

Although only 5'7", he seemed to have the best muscles in the group.

"I'm looking forward to joining the basketball team . . . Do they have a good one?" I asked.

"Pretty damn good, I hear," said Eduardo. "But I like soccer. I like to kick the ball. It relieves my frustrations."

"Maybe I'll join that, too," I said, trying to make a new friend.

As the conversation developed, and more students entered the cafeteria, I learned that Charlie specialized in kung fu. Jean-Marc was more into drama and music. Alistair was top board in the Chess Club.

"I notice the girls sit at different tables from the guys. Why is that?" I asked, now spotting Ling across the room, not showing any sign of recognizing me or our table.

Charlie: "I guess they like to gossip about us!"

We laughed.

But soon, one of the Chinese guys got up from another table and went to talk to Ling as if they were long-time friends. I planned to ask her who he was later that night after school.

"What's it with this school?" I asked. "On my first day, my teacher, Mr. Ching, says Asians are better than Westerners."

Charlie: "Get used to it, man. These dudes are racists. In Canada, nobody would say anything like that."

Alistair: "Chinese have some kind of chip on their shoulder. The other Asians are OK."

Eduardo: "Look out for the Chinese. They can get you into muchas dificultades."

Jean-Marc: "No gum chewing allowed. The laws here suck."

Nobody said anything for a moment.

Then I said,

"Anybody here taking chemistry?"

Charlie said, "Yeah, man. I'll learn how to cook up some fun this term!"

Everyone grinned and laughed again. Then we finished our lunch and filed out.

I headed for Chem class with Charlie McShane. I guess the Chinese part of him gave him a smooth complexion and a movie-star face. His physique was impressive, though at 5'8" I was 2 inches taller.

6

Afternoon Classes

After taking our assigned seats in Chemistry class, as was customary at the school, the teacher introduced me as the newest student, and the rest applauded, including the same 5'6" Chinese guy who had talked to Ling. He must've also taken kung fu, as his physique showed through his tight shirt, even though we all were required to wear the same school uniform with white tops and blue shorts. Sitting behind me, he introduced himself as "Joey Tan."

The teacher, Mr. Wong, then explained that there would be an exam every Monday on what we learned during the week. All homework was due on Thursdays and returned on Fridays. We would go to the lab for experiments on Fridays. Textbooks were then passed out.

We started by trying to memorize the Table of Elements. Mr. Wong put a symbol on the board and asked us to guess which element. He began with H and O, which were easy, and went through all the elements. Then he insisted that we must learn them all by the end of the week. That was our homework.

Next, I reported to the gym class along with the rest of the boys. There were 160 of us. Everyone sat on the bleachers in the main activity room, which was set up for basketball games on one side, gymnastics at the other end. A swimming pool, track, and a soccer field were outside.

Mr. Bennett, the head coach addressed us with a thick English accent. Once again, the new guys had to stand up for recognition. There were 50 of us. He explained that each day we had to strip off our street clothes, put them in our lockers, padlock the lockers, put on our gym uniforms, exercise, then shower, and put back our street clothes. If we liked, we could stay after school for more practice but no later than 6, closing time at the school.

Inquiring which sports we wanted to take, he asked for a show of hands. The taller guys chose basketball, 40 in all, enough for several teams. The leaner ones, also about 40, went out for cross country track or swimming. About 35 muscular but shorter guys, mostly Chinese, volunteered for gymnastics, including both Charlie and Joey. The rest went for soccer, including some of the fatter guys. Some chose two sports. Nobody chose badminton or netball—girls sports, I guess.

Mr. Bennett explained that every day would begin with ten minutes of running laps or tai chi, depending on the weather. Then, properly warmed up, we would report to our favorite sport. He next asked us to form groups corresponding to our chosen specialties.

After that, we went into the locker room. They weighed us and measured our height, and then issued gym uniforms that would fit our different bodies for each sport by height and weight. We then took them home in small blue bags.

We finished the day early. I took a bus toward home. The bus was filled with so many Asian faces, old more than young, that I got sort of dizzy, though they paid no attention to me. En route, I stopped off at a small store operated by an Indian (Tamil) merchant to buy a backpack for the textbooks I got during the day along with a padlock for gym.

7

Home After School

When I got home, Dad was still at work. Yan was preparing dinner while the TV was on, broadcasting news. After saying, "Hi!" I went to my room with a load of books from school, took a shower, and laid down on my bed, resting from the confusion of the day.

When I heard Dad arriving home, I went out to the living room. He said,

"How was it, Jimmy?" while sinking into the sofa opposite the TV, watching sports. "What courses are you taking? How did you like it?"

"There was an assembly of all 400 or so students," I began somewhat mechanically. "Then History, Math, English, Chinese, Chemistry, and finally Gym. I chose basketball, Dad."

Dad: "Good! Did you see Ling? Did you make any new friends, Jimmy?"

"Ling was in the cafeteria, Dad," brightening up as I spoke about her, "but she talked to a Chinese guy who's also in my chemistry class. I lunched with an American Mexican, a Brit, a Canadian, and a French-accented black guy. The Canadian is part-Chinese. Nice guys all."

Dad: "What about the teachers?"

"The gym coach was a Brit. The rest were Chinese . . . Dad, one said Chinese were rising in the world and the West was going down."

"Really?" Dad seemed surprised. "Well, Chinese have been down for centuries, so they have nowhere to go but up. But the West is *not* in decline, Jimmy."

"I agree, Dad."

Then Yan, barely overhearing our conversation, called us to dinner, saying,

"We're not like that in Taiwan. The Singlanders pretend to be better than everyone else."

Dad turned off the TV, and we all sat down at the teakwood dining table.

We filled our mouths with a feast of rice, veggies, and chicken with a tasty hot sauce. Then she brought out cookies, which she baked for dessert with our tea. Nobody drank coffee.

Afterward, we went to the living room and watched TV. There were some local programs, all in English on one channel, and finally the news. President Clinton was up to something, I forget what. There was lots of news about Asia and Europe. Then a rugby game was on the screen. I don't understand rugby, so I got bored.

After about an hour, I excused myself and went to my room to study and do my math homework. I began to doze off around 11 and awoke early the next morning.

In the morning, I had breakfast, got ready for school, and Dad's limo driver Musa drove me to the Paterson Road entrance in very hard rain that stopped about noon and began again after finishing gym class.

8

Basketball Practice, Next Day

Classes were OK on the second day of school. During gym, we had basketball practice inside the gym while the rain poured and poured outside. Team captains from last year chose teams, and we played for an hour before the coach blew the whistle for us to stop. My team had three Americans (me, Ricky Morgan, Bruce Sonnenfeld), one Australian (Josh Carter), and one New Zealander (Colin Edwards). Eduardo asked to join us, as the field was too wet to play soccer, so we kept him on the bench. We were the skins.

The other team, all Asians led by Doug Young, wore tank tops. His teammates were Eric Long, Sangwoon Rhee, Eiji Sakamoto, and Oliver Tuanthai.

We continued after school. A hot game! While we played, Ling and her Chinese girlfriend Vivian came to watch, cheering for us. The tank tops beat us.

After the game, the girls started talking to me.

Ling: "Vivian, this is Jim."

"Hi Vivian. Hi Ling." I pretended that Ling was someone I didn't know very well.

Vivian, acting cute: "You're the new guy, aren't you?"

"Yes," I said, quickly turning my eyes away toward Ling.

Vivian, addressing me: "You sure look very athletic, lah."

Doug Young wandered over while we were chatting:

"Good game, Jim."

We shook hands, using his special handshake.

Doug: "Congratulations for making a lot of free-throw baskets!"

(That was my specialty.)

"Do you guys always win?" I asked coyly.

Doug: "Of course. We play every day after school, and the Asians always beat the white guys. We're hor liao. We're not kiasu!"

(In Singlish, which I was beginning to understand, he was trying to say that they were superior, never afraid of losing a game.)

Jim: "Let's play again tomorrow. I challenge you guys. I bet we'll win tomorrow!"

Doug: "Challenge accepted. But we'll whip your ass again."

"We'll see about that," I boasted.

Then Doug went into the shower.

> Ling, turning her head to me: "I think Doug may want you on his team to try out for varsity."

> "Maybe," I responded coyly. Addressing Vivian, "Say, where can you have fun in Singland?"

> Vivian: "Orchard Road. Lots of restaurants. Bars. Even dance places."

Ling and Vivian then waved goodbye, and I joined the rest of the teams in the locker room. Full of perspiration, I took off my gym clothes and went into the shower.

While showering, I couldn't help but notice that the Chinese guys tended to be much more muscular than those of us from the West. They were even developing 6-packs, including Doug and Joey. Their bodies were smooth and shined like wax. The rest of us Caucasians were beginning to develop hair on our bodies, and we seemed to have more smelly sweat.

I'd always heard that Asians had small ones. But that was definitely not true with the taller guys as I casually looked around, hoping that nobody would notice what my eyes were seeing. I saw they had very little pubic hair unlike me. Some looked at others, making fun, and some even proudly displayed their longevity to other guys. Anyway, nobody was looking at me or mine. After showering, I put my sweaty gym clothes in my backpack to take home for laundry.

As I walked toward the bus stop, Eduardo was going the same way. When I commented on their muscles, he confided,

"I guess gymnastics and kung fu are so much a part of Chinese culture that they start out in elementary school. By the time they reach high school, their muscles are buffed and cut. Let's show 'em how macho we are and they'll envy us!"

We both laughed.

With my previous basketball training in the USA, my arms and shoulders were pretty well developed, and I wasn't fat at all. But some of those Chinese were tall and playing basketball as well. I felt the challenge as an opportunity to improve.

Still waiting for the bus, I couldn't resist asking Eduardo about the lack of hair on their bodies:

"Eduardo, why do they have such smooth, hairless bodies, do you think?"

Eduardo: "In my history class last year, my teacher said that the answer is evolution. He said that when the original Chinese migrated out of Central Asia to present-day China, they had to go through the Gobi Desert. Desiccating winds and intense heat caused many deaths. Sand blowing into pores in hair follicles caused much suffering. The survivors of that ordeal were the ones who lost hair and developed an oily substance to protect their skin. Now, some Chinese believe that they have evolved beyond the other races. I don't believe this tale, but many Chinese do."

"Sounds a little farfetched to me," I said, but we had no other explanation.

Meanwhile, both Eduardo and I were gradually developing little mustaches and hair elsewhere on our teenage bodies.

"Hair makes me feel more macho," Eduardo boasted.

I agreed.

9

The Initiation

The following Monday, as I got more into the groove, knowing what to expect in classes and at the gym, I began to feel at home in Singland. Because Doug's team had other plans that day, I didn't stay after school to continue basketball practice. As I was putting on my clothes after showering, several topless muscular Chinese guys came over to me, looking tough.

"So you are the new whiteboy!" one said. "Well, we must initiate you to become a Mustang, whiteboy!"

Then they grabbed me by my arms and legs, put me down on the floor, held me so I couldn't move, and one lowered my pants to expose my private parts. Another then whipped out a razor and began to shave off my pubic hair.

I objected: "Hey. That's my hair. Leave it alone."

One guy said, "Do you want to be a Mustang, whiteboy?"

I said, "Yes."

"Well, that's how we initiate you, whiteboy."

One of the Chinese guys pulled out a black marking pen and, with artistic aptitude common among those who are accustomed to Chinese calligraphy, began to reproduce the school's cartoonized mustang in the area between my belly button and you know what. When he finished, he smiled and said,

> "Now you can attract the Chinese girls to suck you
> off . . . if you're man enough, whiteboy. They don't
> like hair in their mouths when they suck. Now thank
> us for doing you a favor, whiteboy!"

After I said "Thank you," they let me go, and everyone hugged me. Now, whether I liked it or not, I was a Mustang!

Eduardo saw the whole thing. When we left the gym for the bus stop, he softly advised,

> "They did that to me when I was first here two years
> ago. Don't let it bother you or you'll get into more
> trouble. Don't complain to the administration or the
> teachers. They won't do anything. Boh-chup."

(The Singlish phrase means "Who cares?")

> "Thanks for the advice, pal," I said, while still
> somewhat in shock.

I'd experienced initiations in the Boy Scouts and clubs at my prep school, and indeed Bar Mizvah is a kind of initiation. But I never guessed that there would be one like this. Still, the hugs afterward made me feel accepted.

I realized that the word "whiteboy" was a slur, similar to the word "Chink" that Americans apply derogatorily to Chinese. I didn't like it. But, in time, I had to get used to it. I felt I was a victim of discrimination. Racial discrimination. I would have to find a way to deal with it. I was totally unprepared to be treated with disdain, even in an initiation.

Growing up in Philly, Mom and Dad had told me about anti-Semitism. But this was different. Far more subtle.

10

End of the School Week

The rest of the week went on routinely. Classes were well conducted. I saw Ling sitting on the far side of the cafeteria as usual with her girlfriends. Joey kept talking to her when he got up to put his tray on the conveyer belt.

We lost again in basketball to Doug's Asian team. But the scores got closer each day.

I stayed cool, but my pubic area itched a lot, almost unbearably at first. The itching began to stop on the weekend when new hair had grown out almost as long as before. But now I was a Mustang!

Thursday evening, I called to ask Ling out on a date for the weekend.

> "Are you free to join me Friday night to go to Orchard Road—a meal and a movie?" I inquired.

> "Not Friday. But Saturday, yes," Ling assured.

Slightly disappointedly,

> "I'll meet you around 2 on Saturday. OK?" I hoped she would agree.

"See you then, la," she reassured.

Friday night, Dad and Yan went to a banquet somewhere for his business after she cooked me a burger. I stayed home, bored, so I watched TV and studied a little.

I didn't know what Ling was doing on Friday night. I supposed she would be with her family. When I called her, however, there was no answer. At least, we would date tomorrow.

(Monday, at lunch, Charlie told me that on Friday, she went out with Joey, some girlfriends, and other Chinese dudes to a dance bar. That was OK, I thought. I just got here, and she must have made plans earlier.)

11

Saturday, First Date

Dad had a limo pick up Ling at 2 and bring her to my condo. I was waiting at the lobby for her. Then the limo, driven by Rahman, took us to the cable car for a ride to Sentosa Island beach. Rahman drove away as we boarded. We were on our own. When we got there, we changed into swim clothes and sat down under an umbrella.

"How was your Friday, Jim?" she asked politely.

"Boring," I confessed. "I stayed home and studied. Nothing to do. My parents went somewhere for dinner on business. I microwaved a frozen dinner. How about you?"

Ling: "I went out with some school friends. We all spoke Chinese, so I knew you'd be lost. I'd rather go out just the two of us, lah." She beamed with joy as she spoke.

I told her about growing up in a suburb of Philly near a golf course, the divorce, and how Dad had remarried, with Mom remaining in the USA. I had mentioned the same during my visit in the spring, but she appeared to be hearing it all for the first time.

She talked little about herself. She was born in Singland when the country was still a kind of backwater. But she watched the country grow, as high rises and shopping malls went up and tourists poured into the country from everywhere to shop at bargain prices.

> She confided, "I like foreigners, particularly Americans, for their exuberance."

She was obviously complimenting me, and I responded,

> "I am enchanted by so many beautiful people here
> who are so friendly and smiling. Especially you."

She kind of blushed but hid her emotions from the other people at the beach.

We headed for the water from time to time, showering off the saltwater, and drinking bottled water. She brought a radio, and we began to listen to pop American music. Due to the noise around us, we didn't talk much, just smiled and occasionally dozed off.

When the sun was going down, we went to the changing rooms and put our dressier clothes back on, stashing our wet clothes in our backpacks. Back over the cable car, we took a taxi to Bishun, where we ate at a café near the newly opened Golden Village. Afterward, we went to a movie house and saw *Schindler's List*.

Leaving the movie, she confided,

> "I never knew much about the Jews and the Nazis
> until now."

"There's a long history of persecution of the Jews," I explained, "but never anything as grotesque as with the Nazis."

She then hugged me, and we kissed as never before.

As we left Golden Village, it was dark. Rain was drizzling down, and we kissed again.

"What's planned for tomorrow?" I asked.

"I am always with family on Sunday," she explained. "We visit grandma and take her to dinner. And you?"

"My Dad'll probably take us somewhere. I think he mentioned going to Malacca."

Then we unfurled our umbrellas as the rain started, waited for taxis, and went our separate ways home. It was a dream date. I admired her beauty and modesty. She was even more gorgeous than Yan with her intoxicating eyes and smiles.

Someday, I mused, I would take her to the USA, we would get married, get good jobs, have kids, and live in luxury together. For the first time, I felt that I had planned my whole life.

12

Malacca

Almost every Sunday, Dad took us somewhere. All over Southeast Asia—Kuala Lumpur. Penang. Sarawak. Sabah. Jakarta. Aceh. Sumatra. Bali. Brunei. Bangkok I liked the best. Ling never joined us, as she was always with her family. We usually got home late, and I went right to bed to be ready for school on Monday.

This Sunday, Dad and Mom took me to Malacca. I wished that Ling was along, but I enjoyed the tour. Malacca was once Portuguese and later Dutch, I learned, before the British took over in the colonial days. Then Japan seized control during World War II. In 1945, the British came back. Malaya (now Malaysia) got independence in 1957. Some buildings were very old. We could barely see Indonesia on the other side of the Malacca Strait.

When we got home, Dad turned on the TV for news, but there was a "talk show" instead. Here's what I heard:

> TV moderator Gordon Lau: "Tonight, the topic for discussion is caning, which our courts prescribe for about 1,000 criminals each year. In 1982, the last time there was a poll on caning, only 26 percent of

the people were in favor. Amnesty International, the London human rights organization, says caning is a form of torture contrary to international law. So, gentlemen, should caning be abolished in Singland?"

Senior Minister Low Chai Liang: "In the colonial days of British rule, both caning and whipping with a cat o'-nine-tails were done. We've dropped whipping, but we never gave up caning . . . because it's necessary . . . A state of increasing disorder and defiance of authority can't be checked by leniency. Drastic rules have to be forged to maintain order . . . To adopt any lenient methods would make Singland more dangerous, scare off investment, and force our people to emigrate."

Foreign Minister Krishna Das: "Singland's approach to law and order is based on two basic principles . . . Firstly, we believe the legal system must give maximum protection to the law-abiding majority from a small number of criminals, miscreants, and juvenile delinquents . . . Secondly, arrested persons have the right to due process of law. But when found guilty, offenders must be punished sufficiently so they and others will be deterred from repeating the offense . . . No one who is caned will ever want to be caned again."

Home Affairs Minister Henry Cheng: "Unlike some other societies which may tolerate acts of vandalism, Singland has its own standards of social order . . . Nobody takes any joy in carrying out these strict punishments, be it imprisonment, caning, or execution. But they have to be carried out. Laws will only be effective if penalties for flouting them are strict. Because of our tough laws against anti-social crimes, we're able to keep Singland orderly and relatively crime-free . . . We don't have a situation where acts of vandalism are commonplace, as in New York, where even police cars are vandalized . . . If we give up caning, we'll have chaos."

Parliamentarian Tung Tai Yim: "In America, they seem to have lost the feeling that people are responsible for their own behavior. Here, there is still a sense of personal responsibility. If you do something against the law, you bring shame not only to yourself but to your family. So, we only cane the most hardened criminals."

Information Minister Soon Keong Ong: "We've always had caning, and we wouldn't have safety in Singland without caning."

Deputy Prime Minister Low Heng Tao: "Because of strict enforcement of the law, everyone in the world should know that if you live in Singland, your life, limb, and properties will be quite safe."

As the TV reporter asked more questions, Dad turned to another channel for news, weather, and sports.

It was a wonderful day of adventure, thanks to Dad. After watching a tennis match, I crashed.

13

A Tournament

After four weeks, we got deeper into our studies. History finally got beyond China. Math progressed to locus problems. We finished *Great Expectations* and went on to *Crime and Punishment*. In Chinese class, my vocabulary increased to 350 words of calligraphy. During chemistry experiments, a couple of students miscalculated and caused minor explosions. Gym got more competitive as October approached.

Coach Bennett was eager for contests during the Hari Raya Haji Festival, a three-day holiday when Muslims celebrate those who go on the annual pilgrimage to Mecca.

He had two soccer teams compete one day, followed by a swimming contest the next day. Swimmers competed individually one day and in relays the next. The gymnasts also competed one day, followed by the kungfu guys putting on exhibitions the next. The coach selected four basketball teams and asked us to compete. Our team, the C team, easily defeated the D team. The next day, we played Doug's A team, which had beaten the B team, but we played to a draw. There was even a Chess Club match.

All contests were announced in advance to the rest of the island so anyone could attend, sit on the sidelines, and cheer.

During games with umpires, I sometimes heard spectators yell out "Referee kayu!" when they didn't like their calls. They were saying that the referees were "blockheads."

Ling and Vivian sat in the bleachers during basketball games. During breaks, I went over to them to say "Hi!" and they encouraged us to win. They also attended other sporting events, including the gymnastics contest, where Joey actioned ("showed off" in Singlish).

There was a lot of aggressive talking in the locker room as we changed into and out of our uniforms for the various contests. We were all fired up.

The coach was right! With competition before spectators from around the island, we all did our very best. Some guys made school records, and we all improved.

14

Bisexuality

Next week was midterm exam week. I studied hard for all the courses over the weekend after the tournament. I was having the most trouble with Chinese. Ling came over to our penthouse and helped me a lot.

Most guys skipped gym to study. I did a little basketball practice to calm my nerves on Wednesday. When I went into the almost empty locker room, I thought I heard two guys showering. But when I looked, I saw one Japanese basketball guy (Eiji) from our chemistry class on his knees sucking Joey. I tried not to look. I waited until they finished and then took my shower alone.

After putting on my clothes, I walked out and found Joey outside. I whispered,

> "Are you guys gay?"

He quickly corrected me,

> "By no means. You Americans have it all wrong. Here in Singland, we are bisexual. We mostly go with girls, but why not have some fun with a guy, too?

You Westerners think everything is black and white, either gay or straight. Not here in Asia. It's healthy to have sex with someone you like. Eiji was doing it with me because he was a blur at math. He was thanking me for my help this weekend in showing him how to solve his calculus problems for his exam. Everything in Singland has a price! He might do it for me someday in another class if I find something chim. But I'm smarter." Echoing a popular song, "Guys just wanna have fun!"

(To be "blur" in Singlish is to be confused. "Chim" is something that is hard to understand.)

"If you ever want to give me service, Jim, let me know!"

"No way, dude. I'm straight, through and through," I snapped.

"Have it your way, dude!" he fired back . . . Then calmly, "But let's have some other fun I'm planning."

"What do you mean?" I quizzed.

"Well, a group of us guys go to the rich houses on the island and collect things that are thrown away. Sort of a treasure hunt. We take them home and put them on the walls of our rooms. How would you like to join us Sunday night?"

"Sure. I have nothing to do then. I'm game. Where do we meet?"

I didn't realize exactly what he was talking about. But on such a cozy place, what else was there to do on free nights? Dad was going out of town that weekend.

> "We'll meet at Bojangles in the shopping mall at 170 Upper Bukit Timah Road around 6:30. Take a bus and meet us!"

I nodded "Yes."

> Joey: "See you then!" ("Bukit Timah" means "tin hill." Bojangels was a popular bar.)

> "Cool. I'll check at home," I said semi-cautiously. "If I can, I'll make it."

I didn't realize at the time that Joey was trying to set me up. I thought he was just being friendly to take the edge off the fact that we both were courting Ling. I was *so* naïve.

15

Friday at the Disco, Saturday on a Date

As we were becoming buddies, I talked Eduardo into going out to the Zouk disco, a former warehouse, on Friday night so we could see the girls, since Ling would be busy with her friends again that night.

After we entered, they were playing *Flashdance*. I shared with Eduardo,

> "Wow! This is the fanciest disco I've ever seen . . . with the prettiest girls. I'd enjoy coming here every Friday night . . . There's Ling and Vivian!"

> Eduardo: "Avoid the Asian señoritas. Their boyfriends think they own 'em."

> "I'll take my chances," I said. "I'm interested in Ling. I've been dating her on Saturdays."

> Eduardo: "But she's Joey's ger." (ger = girl)

"Really?" I was incredulous, "I can't believe that. How long have they been seeing each other?"

Eduardo: "It's a family matter. Their parents want them to marry someday. So, they date on Fridays. But I'm not sure they're really in love."

"We've already kissed. Ling and I. We're serious."

Then they played *Girls Just Want to Have Fun* or some other hit dance song from 1983.

Eduardo: "Vivian keeps giving me the eye."

I got up to dance with Ling. Eduardo chose Vivian. The Chinese guys looked annoyed when white guys found some Chinese girls and danced with them.

We had a great time, dancing and drinking all night! But our ears seemed deaf when we left. The music was *so* loud.

(Later, I got a DVD of the hits from that year, and some seemed very appropriate at the time—*Let's Dance, Jump (For My Love), Tonight I Celebrate My Love, The Politics of Dancing, Love Is a Battlefield, Uptown Girl, Karma Chameleon, China Girl.* But others seemed to predict what would happen next—*Maniac, Borderline, On the Dark Side.* Pop music isn't the same now.)

As usual, on Saturday, I dated Ling. This Saturday, instead of Sentosa, we did a walking tour of the local university campus. Afterward, we went to eat and see a movie, *Dragon: The Bruce Lee Story.* I didn't mention that I'd heard she was also being pursued by Joey. I didn't want to detract from our relationship.

As we left the cinema with other patrons, I asked

"Did you like the movie?"

Ling: "I especially liked when Bruce Lee showed off his muscles, la!"

Then I flexed my left biceps, boasting,

"Any bigger than mine?"

Ling: "Can you show your right biceps?"

"Like, everything, babe," I said seductively.

We kissed.

"I'll take you home now," I promised.

Then we got into a taxi, which drove through the night lights on Orchard Road, with a few prostitutes parading along the sidewalk on the east side. After dropping her off, I stayed in the cab, which took me home.

16

Treasure Hunting Sunday

The next day, Sunday, Dad had to go out of town again. I decided to join Joey for the treasure hunt. Saying goodbye to Yan, I headed for Bukit Timah after dinner. When I got there at 7, Joey was there with several guys—Alistair, Bruce, Eduardo, Eiji, and Oliver.

Joey: "OK, guys, let's hunt for traffic signs. A lot fall down, and many are so loose they can be pried off the poles. The one who collects the most signs gets the prize."

Bruce: "What's the prize?

Eduardo: "The prize is to have the most signs."

We all laughed.

We strolled up the road, each taking different roads. We looked inside trashcans and for anything that fell on the street or roadsides and agreed to go back to the starting place by 9 with at least one item each.

No moon was out, so the hunt was in the dark except for houselights and streetlamps. We hiked up the road and went across the side streets, starting with empty backpacks and filling them with anything that looked good.

I didn't find much in the trash bins. Just junk and paper. A "One Way" street sign had fallen, so I picked it up and showed it to the guys afterward at 9, when we quit.

> Joey: "That's good, Jim. Take it home and put it on your wall as a trophy. I pried off a couple of hubcaps, lah."

> Alistair: "I found a street sign." Displaying a worn-out "Upper Bukit Timah Road" sign, he guessed, "I think this sign was blown down in the big rain on Thursday."

> Oliver: "I got a used looseleaf notebook in the trash with business papers. I'll throw away the papers and maybe use the notebook for school."

> Eiji: "It felt creepy. I'm not coming back."

> Joey: "Spoil sport! Goondu! We don't want you if you don't enjoy yourself . . . Everyone else, let's show our signs to our friends tomorrow. Shall we do this again next Sunday, guys?"

("Goondu" is Singlish for idiot, kind of the opposite of "guru.")

All of us but Eiji nodded "Yes," and we went our separate ways. When I got home, I put my sign on the wall in my room and went to bed before Dad got back.

17

Monday After the Hunt

After morning classes, we went to lunch. Everyone at my table was there as usual.

Charlie: "Jim, are you getting more serious with Ling?"

I ventured,

"Great. But she's also Joey's girl. So far."

Eduardo: "Go for it, man. Outscore those Asian dudes! Don't let them claypot you."

(To "claypot" in Singlish is to lose, the opposite of jackpot.)

Alistair, sitting down with a tray, unloaded and then opened his backpack, displaying a street sign,

"How would you like some traffic signs to decorate your rooms?"

Jean-Marc: "Is that a violation of the law here? I don't want to make any la sai." (He said he didn't want to cause any trouble.)

Alistair: "So what? I have diplomatic immunity because of my dad. He's just been transferred to Sweden, so I'm leaving next month."

Then he passed the sign around to everyone at the table but Jean-Marc, who pulled his hands back to decline the gift.

Eduardo: "We'll miss you. Hasta la vista!"

Charlie: "How did you get those signs?

I then explained,

"I went out scavenger hunting with Joey. We looked for traffic signs that fell down and other stuff."

Then I pulled the One Way sign from my backpack to show them all.

Joey, getting up from another table, took his tray to the conveyor belt, and then walked over to join our table.

"I see Alistair's and Jim's showing you some of last night's loot. Next Sunday night, let's have some more fun together. Let's collect more traffic signs." Addressing Charlie, "Want to come along and be one of the tough guys of the International School?"

Encouraging Charlie, I said,

"There's really nothing much to do in Singland, is there? It's so boring here."

Charlie, giving thumbs up, "I also have diplomatic immunity. Sort of."

Eduardo: "Que buena idea. I'm game."

Jean-Marc: "No way, man. If a black dude does something different here, they go ballistic."

Joey: "OK, you guys. Meet at the corner of Orchard Road and Tanglin at 6 p.m. Sunday night. We'll go to Upper Bukit Timah, where all the rich people live."

Then Joey gave a special handshake to everyone except Jean-Marc. We finished lunch and went back to class—Chemistry and Gym for me.

I joined the guys from time to time after that. Every Sunday night when Dad didn't take Yan and me on a trip, that is. My room began to fill up with road signs, and I began to understand the geography of the island a little better each time.

Dad and Yan didn't object at first, though later Dad asked me to stop cluttering my room. But I felt I was accumulating a collection of "pop art."

18

Varsity Basketball

Tuesday afternoon, I was looking forward to basketball. The A team again played the C team, this time with the Asian as skins, the Caucasians wearing shirts. While Ling and Vivian watched, the game ended with the Caucasians yelling victoriously. All perspiring, Doug and I talked while the rest of the teams went to the locker room:

> Doug: "You guys played great, Jim. That's our first claypot in a long time."

> "Thanks, Doug, but you guys may win next time," I said calmly.

> Doug: "Don't be so modest. Anyway, the coach has agreed to put you on the varsity team, so both of us will play together against the other high schools in town."

> "Wow! As a team," I predicted, "we'll beat the other schools."

Then we stopped to talk to Ling and Vivian.

Ling: "So Jim tipped the balance against you guys. What do you say about that, la?"

Doug: "We'll beat them next time. But Jim's on the varsity team with me, so the school may be league champs this year."

Vivian teased: "Imagine that. One American and you're already thinking of big things, la!"

Doug: "Well, he isn't so big in the shower."

We all laughed.

Then Doug and I entered the locker room as the other guys had just finished and were putting on their street clothes. At 6' he was the tallest Chinese guy I ever met. With really big deltoids (shoulders), he was a damn good basketball player. He maneuvered his way on the court like a ballet star.

When I got home, I told my parents I made varsity. I called Mom in Pennsylvania to tell her, too. They were all very pleased with me.

Dad said he noticed my grades were slipping and cautioned me not to go out on weekends too much but instead to stick to my books.

But basketball was my dream sport, and I enjoyed dating and playing around town. I was becoming more fluent in Singlish than in the Chinese taught at school.

19

Another Sunday Night of Vandalism

As Sunday nights continued, the guys got more daring.

On a darkly lit side street, Bruce met with Joey, Charlie, Eduardo, and Oliver. (Alistair had already left the country.) With the weather report predicting rain, I decided to practice my basketball shooting instead—under the watchful eye of the ever-present gym camera.

As I was told later by Bruce and Charlie, Joey brought along spraypaint. He wanted to spray some of the cars white, thinking it was a harmless prank because the paint was easily removable and wouldn't cause permanent damage.

Oliver brought a brick.

Bruce says he wanted no part of paint spraying or brick-throwing. Instead, he brought eggs.

Charlie and Eduardo stuck to picking up signs because they didn't want to go too far.

This night, Joey and Oliver paired off, according to Eduardo. They began to mess up cars, spraypainting the fanciest cars—the Bentleys, especially. Joey also spraypainted down a line of 18 Mercedes.

Oliver threw a brick at the right window of a Mercedes, while Bruce threw eggs at other cars.

The rest found traffic signs and two taxi license plates, put them in their backpacks, and wandered off.

Joey and Oliver also interchanged license plates and sawed- off Mercedes emblems.

Later, Bruce overheard that Joey was disturbed because I was dating Ling and that Joey said,

> "That bastard!" referring to me. "He'll get what he
> deserves, thinking he's better than us Chinese. Let's
> up the ante, cause damage, and then blame it on
> him!"

Oliver evidently went along. Joey had some kind of control over Oliver—a debt or something.

20

Cafeteria, Monday

Students were eating as usual, Ling sitting with her girlfriends.

Joey, going to our table after he finished his meal and bused his tray, asked,

"Did you enjoy sign hunting last night, guys?"

Charlie: "A lot of fun!"

Joey: "Let's do it again next Sunday night, guys."

Like a fool, I said,

"Sure!"

Eduardo: "What else is there to do on this island?"

Charlie: "No. I've got some studying to do."

Joey: "How about the rest of you guys?"

Jean-Marc: "No way, man. What if police find out?"

Joey: "They won't. They're hardly ever around."

Charlie, Eduardo, and I shrugged our shoulders.

We were such fools. We didn't realize that real people lived in those houses and owned those automobiles. Rich people. Important people—people with connections in high places.

Government and politics were not taught at the International School. Most Singlanders left politics to the politicians and voted for the ruling party. The government, lacking opposition, could wield absolute power. And often did, as we soon found out.

21

Bukit Timah

The following Sunday, we met again at the beginning of the Upper Bukit Timah residential area—Joey, Bruce, Eduardo, Oliver, and me.

While the rest went up to the houses, Joey asked me to go with him. Then he let me have it:

"Lay off my ger, aiyoh whiteboy."

(He was calling me a "filthy" white guy.)

Standing my ground, ready to defend myself in case of a punch,

"It's her decision, not yours, Joey. Are you jealous?"

Joey: "You stupid American. It *isn't* her decision. In Asia, men tell women what to do. Lay off or else."

"Or else what?" I nearly cursed.

Joey: "Don't fuck with me."

"I have as much right to date girls as you," I protested. "Don't get so excited."

Joey: "Your last date with Ling was your last."

"We'll see about that," I thundered.

As our voices got louder, I could see porchlights come on two of the houses. They were probably looking at us to see what all the commotion was about.

Next, Joey stormed down the hill away from the houses.

Some of the rest of the treasure hunters heard us, astonished at the altercation.

I shrugged my shoulders and walked downhill right afterward. That, I thought, was my final treasure hunt!

The rest of the guys evidently ignored our departure and continued treasure hunting.

22

The Arrest

What I didn't realize was that the police knew about our antics over the past weeks. Owners of the cars were extremely angry about the spraypainting, and they were very well connected. The previous Monday, one of them had telephoned the Home Affairs Minister, whom he knew personally, demanding that the government stop the mischief.

According to police records that later came to light, there were more than 30 secret societies of young Singlanders roaming the streets, carrying large knives, engaging in shoplifting, and breaking out in fights in front of crowded shopping centers. Now we'd engaged in five nights of vandalism in a residential area. The fear voiced by the government on TV all week was that local youth were becoming as unruly as Western youth.

A trap was set. After dark, about 7:30 p.m., police wearing plainclothes sat in unmarked parked cars strategically placed throughout Upper Bukit Timah. Their instructions were to question anyone suspicious and to arrest any vandals caught in the act.

One of the residents, who saw Joey and me quarreling, alerted the police that we were running away. Two uniformed police were waiting for us at the bus stop below.

"Why you running, boys?" an officer named Fong asked brusquely.

Joey: "We're just jogging, officer."

The other officer named Chua:

"You boys been throwing eggs at the cars up there?"

I said, "No, sir."

To Joey: "Did you see anyone vandalize these cars?"

"No, sir," Joey said, trying to keep cool.

Then the first officer took Joey to the other side of the road, out of earshot of me and the other officer. Chua, after questioning me, raised his voice and demanded,

"You know more than you say. Either we arrest you or you tell us who did it."

"Well, some of our classmates at the International School might know something," I said tentatively.

"Who? Give us their names."

I refused, shrugging my shoulder.

"You must come down to the police station for a complete statement of what you saw." Making a sign to Chua, Fong said, "You and your friend are under arrest."

Joey then said, "Wa-liao! Alamak! Jia lat!"

(In English, he was saying "Good grief! Oh my god! We're in trouble!") At school, he had been very confident. Now, he was terrified. We both were.

The police then handcuffed us, put us in their police car, and drove to Tanglin Police Station. After booking us, they had us empty out our pockets and surrender our backpacks. They put us in adjacent cells.

Soon, the rest of our group arrived and were locked up. Bruce, in the next holding cell, had his shirt bloodied from an apparent nosebleed and was holding a bloodied handkerchief to his nose.

Still shaken by the arrest, I asked,

> "What happened to you, Bruce?"

> Bruce: "Police arrested me, saying I was a terrorist. They punched me in the nose, smacked my ear, and hit me with a billyclub." Pointing to his left ear, "I still can't hear out of my ear."

> "Terrorist?" I exclaimed.

Then Bruce hushed me from saying anything more.

> Joey said "no bao toh." (Don't tattle.)

23

Initial Interrogation

As an American, I expected to have the police read my rights. But they didn't. I expected that I could call Dad to bring a lawyer. That didn't happen either. Instead, one by one, we were escorted under handcuffs into separate interrogation rooms. I don't know exactly what happened to the others, because they were too scared to reveal what they encountered, but I will never forget my experience of being questioned in a Singland jail.

When I entered the interrogation room, a Chinese officer with a badge named "Lee," motioned for me to sit on one side of a table and left the room. A few minutes passed. A Tamil officer named "Devanesan" entered and sat on the other side.

Devanesan: "James Freeman?"

"That's me."

"An eyewitness reports you spraypainted 18 cars at 8 p.m. last Sunday. Just sign a statement admitting your guilt and you can go home."

"But I was practicing basketball then. Watch the video on the camera at the gym."

Devanesan: "Bullshit, terok whiteboy! You were koping, pai kia. You're a terrorist."

("Terok" means difficult or troublesome. To "kope" is to steal. A "pai kia" is a hooligan.)

"I want a lawyer."

Devanesan: "Lawyers aren't allowed here. This is a police station. Confess or we'll keep you here indefinitely until you confess your terrorism."

"Check out my story, sir. My playing was videotaped. I'm *not* a terrorist."

Officer Lee came into the room and blurted out

"Our eyewitness also saw you steal traffic signs. We can go to your room at home to verify his story. Tell the truth now and we'll go easy on you, whiteboy."

"Is possession of a discarded street sign something bad?"

Devanesan: "I'll ask the questions, whiteboy. Did you get any?"

"One was a gift from Alistair, my British friend who recently left Singland. I have nothing more to say until I see a lawyer."

Lee: "And you spraypainted cars last Sunday, too!"

"No, sir. I was playing basketball."

As both officers left the room, Lee yelled,

> "Confess to spraypainting or else! Now when I come back, I want you to see you stripped of all your clothes. Put them in a pile near the door, terok whiteboy. I want to see your white kar chng when I come back!"

(He demanded to see my white ass.)

Devanesan released my handcuffs so I could do so. They slammed and locked the door as they left.

Strip? The room suddenly got colder. I didn't take off my clothes. What was going on? I was confused and frightened. A few streets signs seemed harmless, and spraypainting wasn't my thing. I wondered how the other guys were doing, and I was getting colder and colder.

Officer Lee came back into the room and saw me fully clothed, ordering,

> "Strip, whiteboy, or I'll have police come in and tear off your clothes so you won't have any left. Immediately! Chop-chop!"

I complied. Lee then left the room. When the door opened again, two uniformed Malay officers grabbed me, pushed me toward the wall, and tied my hands to two hooks at arm's length on the wall, spreadeagled, with my chest to the wall, exposing my back and butt.

Lee returned. Spanking my butt hard,

> "Are you ready to confess, terrorist?"

"I'm not saying anything more."

"You can stay there the rest of your life for all I care. We're sending police to your residence to seize any evidence we can find. Meanwhile, you can stay like that, whiteboy! We have a camera focused on your dirty white ass!"

Then he left the room. It was so cold that I began to piss. I couldn't hold back anymore!

24

Search and Seizure

On hearing of my arrest from Charlie, who'd been released, Ling called my parents, but she didn't know much about why or where I was. My father called a lawyer at his place of business but had no details to tell him other than that I was in jail.

Soon, two uniformed Chinese officers went to our condo to search. As Dad later reported, they first asked the doorman if I got home the previous Sunday with paint on my clothes. Then they knocked hard on the door of our penthouse, startling my parents. Opening the door, Dad demanded to see a warrant for the search and wanted to know the charges against me and where I was held. They gave him a warrant and asked where my room was.

My room, which was a bit messy, with my basketball uniform lying on a chair. The two officers entered and collected various signs (including a "Watch Your Step" sign from a bus, a "Not For Hire" sign from a taxi, a "No Smoking" sign, a "No Exit" sign, and various signboards). They put them into a black polyethylene bag along with some flags and firecrackers that I had been saving for New Years. Next, they searched my clothes in the closet for any sign of paint. They opened the drawers of my desk and dresser, pulling everything out to the floor. Evidently, there was a tattered flag on the floor in my closet, so that was also put into the bag, while Dad watched the operation.

One officer asked if there was any spraypaint in the apartment. Yan answered No.

Meanwhile, Dad read the warrant, which charged me with vandalism. He threatened to call the American Embassy and demanded to know where I was being held.

> One officer said, "Tanglin. You can't see him. Calling
> the embassy will do no good on a Sunday night."

They demanded my passport, and Dad said it was in a safe deposit box at the bank. They wanted to know which bank and evidently arranged to confiscate my passport that night.

When the officers left, Dad got on the phone to call the American Embassy, which sent Consul George Williamson to Tanglin to demand my release.

25

More Interrogation

Consul Williamson taxied from the Embassy to Tanglin to get me released. He demanded to pay bail, but I hadn't seen a judge to set bail. He was told that I would be released as soon as the police got hold of my passport. He asked for more details, but they only told him that official charges hadn't been brought against me. He reported back to Dad and left.

Meanwhile, I was still tied up, naked, in a very cold room.

Lee, entering the interrogation room, said,

> "We've just come from your room at home, asshole. You've defaced our country's flag."

He then spanked my left butt.

> "We found lots of street signs, too. We also know you're also guilty of spraypainting!"

I protested, "I know nothing about any spraypainting."

"You lie, whiteboy. Confess now or you'll spend the rest of your life here in the nude, tied to the wall. We don't tolerate terrorism."

"I can't confess something I didn't do. I want a lawyer."

As Officer Devanesan came into the room, Officer Lee said,

"I'm finished with this dickhead. Take him to a cell for the night." Talking to me, "Unless you agree to sign a statement now, confessing you spraypainted 18 cars."

I shook my head "No."

Then Devanesan untied me, ordered me to dress, and escorted me to my cell.

Jail was my home for the night along with the other guys. I spread the word,

"Don't confess or sign any statement." They nodded agreement with their heads down. I didn't know they would eventually sign statements, and so would I.

I couldn't believe this was happening to me. Surely, my parents would know everything by now. Although I didn't know it at the time, Dad asked a lawyer from his business to get me released, but the lawyer instead urged my parents to go to the American Embassy first thing the next morning. I tried to sleep, but I was too nervous and upset. The door from the police desk to inside the jail was open, and I could faintly hear the TV:

News Anchor Gordon Lau: "In local news, police arrested 5 International School students yesterday for their part in a 5-week spree of vandalism, including 3 Americans . . . Because there were so many Americans, we interviewed 2 government officials for an explanation."

Parliamentarian Tung Tai Yim: "In the West, if an individual commits a crime, society is blamed. There's no demand for individual accountability. This is misplaced compassion. Our almost crime-free society has come about partly because we always ask individuals to differentiate between right and wrong. It's the certainty and severity of punishment that keep a safe and orderly society."

Senior Minister Low Chai Liang: "For the West, the individual is more important than society. For Asians, the society has always been more important than the individual . . . In America, a driver is hauled out of his truck and has his head smashed by rioters, but the rioters get off. A woman cuts off her husband's penis and she gets off . . . In the United States, everyone expects to be protected by the law from the serious consequences of their actions. Not here in Singland."

Then the police shut the door, and I couldn't hear any more. I figured they were bluffing, anyway. I lay down and tried to sleep but couldn't until I saw that everyone else was sleeping. Then I guess I dozed off.

26

American Embassy

The next morning, my parents went to the American Embassy, seeking help. I learned from Dad that they talked to a young Chargé d'Affaires, William Warren, who promised to try to get me released. He said that under the local law, they're only allowed visitors after two days when they have a court hearing. After making a call to someone, Warren indicated that the police were probably still holding me to force me to confess.

Warren reported that there had been a spree of vandalism in Bukit Timah, including spraypainting. He said the government was enforcing the Vandalism Act, which passed in 1966. The aim of the law, I learned later, was to criminalize political graffiti and the stealing of government property. But that law was now being applied to simple pranks, like the ones that I had been doing with my friends.

He cautioned that when the top men in the country want to stop something, they aren't gentle. He called the government the Singlish Clobbering Machine. He indicated that a diplomatic protest had been drafted and soon would be delivered to the Foreign Ministry, since an American bystander saw a member of the police assault one of the boys, unprovoked, on a street in Upper Bukit Timah.

Using diplomatic protest, they would find out where the orders came from to arrest me and then pressure those higher up to release me. He would personally request to see me based on a well-established principle of international law that nationals in a foreign jail had the right to be represented by consular officials from their embassies.

Otherwise, he urged, I should have a lawyer. But not just any lawyer—a barrister with experience dealing with the government. He then called the law firm of Derek Savundranayagan and Stanley Suriyakumaran.

My parents thanked Warren, and then went to the office of the two barristers to get representation for me. After paying a legal retainer and agreeing to an hourly legal fee, they both agreed to represent me when charges were to be read against me in court on Tuesday.

27

Jail Visits

The embassy got permission to send Chargé d'Affaires Warren to visit that afternoon. He accompanied Yan. Dad was at work. When they arrived, they asked for Prosecutor Henry Au. The police receptionist cleared them and then waited to talk to Mr. Au. After the prosecutor came out to greet them, they identified themselves and asked to see me.

Au, a bespectacled rotund man in his fifties who appeared stressed, told them I admitted to possessing stolen property, but he still had some questions to ask me about other matters. He would let them see me but wouldn't release me until my barrister would write a letter, apologizing for my behavior.

Then Au escorted both Warren and Yan back to the receptionist, who admitted them to see me. I was accompanied from my cell by a prison guard to a window with a chair. They were on the other side of the window, seated.

Tears coming down her face, Yan cried, "Jimmy!"

"Yan!" (sobbing) "My life is over! Who's this man?"

Warren: "I'm from the American Embassy. We'll get you out soon. The Prosecutor just wants a letter of apology from the lawyers whom your parents have hired."

Brightening up, I smiled, "Great! How soon?"

Yan: "Soon, Jimmy."

After Yan asked me about the lousy prison food, the police receptionist came in, saying.

"Time's up."

Then she led them to the exit of the police station.

What I didn't know is that the prosecutor decided to lie about releasing me, hoping to extort an apology from a barrister. The letter would be used as an official admission of my guilt. The court hearing was to occur the following morning.

The guard in the jail then took me to the prosecutor's office.

Au: "You have to be in court tomorrow, so we're keeping you here for another night."

I humbly protested, "But I was told that I'd be released soon."

Au: "It will be easier on you if you confess to spraypainting those cars."

When he presented a statement for me to sign, I exclaimed,

"Did you check the security camera at my school gym? That will clear me." I refused to sign.

"No," Au said firmly, "Any evidence will be presented at trial, not now."

⁘⁘⁘

Later that night, Dad, Ling, and barrister Suriyakumaran came to visit me. Ling just smiled at me and waved but was quiet.

Dad: "This is Mr. Suriya, Jimmy" unable to pronounce his name. "He'll be representing you in court tomorrow."

"Su-ri-ya-KU-ma-ran," he corrected.

"Nice to meet you," I said politely.

I didn't even try to pronounce such a long name.

Suriyakumaran: "Have you made any confessions, James?"

Sheepishly, "I told them I got a street sign from a friend who left the country. That's all."

Suriyakumaran: "Don't say anything more, even in court. I'll do the talking for you."

"OK," I said as if doomed to silence.

To Suriyakumaran: "Why do they keep calling me a terrorist?"

Suriyakumaran: "The original law about vandalism was meant to stop political opponents who defaced government buildings with graffiti. 'Terrorism' is difficult to define legally, so they have criminalized supposed acts of terrorism, such as vandalism. They equate vandalism with terrorism. They can't seem to distinguish between the two, even though vandalism can occur without political motivations."

Then Dad asked, "How are you holding out, son?"

"I've been tortured," I whispered so the nearby guard couldn't hear.

Dad: "I'll tell the American Embassy, and we'll get you out ASAP, Jimmy."

"Thanks, Dad."

Then Dad mumbled something to the lawyer, who was a "barrister"— that is, the kind of attorney who pursues cases in court. (The other kind of lawyer, a solicitor, is the one who accepts clients in the first place.)

They left, and I was taken back to my cell. At least, the police guard, Jerry Teuku, was polite as he locked me up again.

(I later learned that Warren at the U.S. Embassy did take up the claim of abuse with government authorities, who then sent a physician to examine me in jail later that night. The report revealed no evidence of physical abuse, so the complaint was dropped.)

28

Arraignment

Early Tuesday morning, I was put into a van and hauled to the basement of the court along with the other four guys who'd been arrested. A Gurkha named Gajbahadur Rai was at the entrance on the side of the court; he opened a trap door so we could walk up into court. It was a British-type courtroom. The room was spotless and had plenty of wood paneling. A Singland flag was prominently displayed. The spectator gallery was separated by a wooden railing, and the seats looked like church pews. Seated were a Court Bailiff, Court Clerk, and a Court Stenographer. Prosecutor Au and barristers were at adjacent tables.

The Bailiff accompanied me to join Bruce, Eduardo, Joey, and Oliver, who were seated to one side near a Witness Box. In the gallery were the boys' parents, nervous, as well as Ling, Vivian, and 12 teenage courtroom spectators, mostly girlfriends of the accused and other students from school.

Court Bailiff (as the Judge entered the courtroom):

"All rise."

Everyone stood and bowed slightly toward the Judge. The Judge walked over to his seat and sat down.

Judge Julian De Silva: "You may be seated."

Everyone sat down but the Court Clerk.

Court Clerk: "Case number 93125694. The People Versus Bruce Sonnenfeld."

The Court Bailiff asked Bruce to stand up in the Witness Box.

Prosecutor Au: "Your Honor, the people are not ready to charge the defendant at this time."

Judge, banging the gavel: "Case deferred. Mr. Sonnenfeld, you are free to go."

Court Clerk: "Case number 93125695. The People Versus Eduardo Ramírez."

The Court Bailiff also asked Eduardo to stand up in the Witness Box.

Prosecutor Au: "Your Honor, the people are not ready to charge the defendant at this time."

Judge, banging the gavel: "Case deferred. Mr. Ramírez, you are free to go."

Court Clerk: "Case number 93125696. The People Versus Joseph Tan."

Joey then stood up and walked over to stand in the Witness Box.

Court Clerk: "The charges are 16 counts of vandalism, 5 counts of malicious mischief, and 15 counts of receiving stolen property."

Judge: "How do you plead, Mr. Tan?"

Wilfred Keong, Tan's attorney: "Your Honor, although Joseph Tan signed a confession admitting to all counts, he has repudiated his confession on the grounds that it was extorted from him by police torture. Accordingly, we plead not guilty."

Prosecutor Au, addressing the judge: "There's absolutely no basis for the defense attorney's claim. The confession was provided willingly."

Judge: "The confession is admissible. Defendant, with a plea of not guilty, must stand trial," banging the gavel. "What bail do you recommend, Mr. Prosecutor?"

Prosecutor Au: "No bail. I recommend that he be retained in jail until trial."

Joey's attorney Keong: "I object. He's not a flight risk."

Judge: "Objection overruled. Remand him into custody."

The trap door opened, and the Bailiff escorted Joey down the ramp.

Court Clerk: "Case number 93125697. The People Versus Oliver Tuanthai.

Oliver moved over to stand in the Witness Box.

Prosecutor Au: "Your Honor, the people are not ready to charge the defendant at this time."

Judge, banging the gavel: "Case deferred. Mr. Tuanthai, you are free to go."

Court Clerk: "Case number 93125702. The People Versus James Alan Freeman. The charges are 16 counts of vandalism, 5 counts of malicious mischief, 15 counts of receiving stolen property, and 1 count of possessing firecrackers."

The Court Bailiff asked me to stand up in the Witness Box, and I did so.

Judge: "How do you plead, Mr. Freeman?"

Barrister Savundranayagan: "Mr. Freeman pleads Not Guilty."

Judge: "What is your bail recommendation, Mr. Prosecutor?"

Prosecutor Au: "No bail. I recommend that he be retained in jail until trial."

Savundranayagan: "I object. He is not a flight risk. This is the first offense. My client was assured that he would be released today."

Judge: "Who made that assurance?"

> Savundranayagan: "Prosecutor Au asked for me to write a letter of apology for the conduct of my client."

(I knew nothing about an apology but suspected that there was a trick of some sort by the prosecutor.)

> Au: "I never received any such apology. Besides, he's already confessed to one of the charges."

> Savundranayagan: "Still, the government has his passport. Why hold him for only one confessed charge?"

> Judge: "Objection overruled. Remand Mr. Freeman into custody, awaiting trial."

> Court Clerk: "That's all for this morning, Your Honor."

> Judge: "Court is adjourned." As the judge left the courtroom, everyone stood and bowed.

As I was escorted by the same Gurkha guard down the ramp to join Joey, I saw Dad talking to the prosecutor in an agitated manner while Bruce Sonnenfeld was handing a note to Yan.

The note, which I later read, explained: "We were being treated terribly. We slept on a moldy mattress, with ants all around us. The investigators tried by force to pry confessions from us for things we hadn't done. They punched, kicked, slapped, and whipped most of us. They are trying to bust us for almost everything."

I saw Yan burst into tears as she read the note.

We were then hauled back to jail. While en route, Joey and I said nothing. But we pointed our tongues at the court building.

The driver, a young Malay woman named Aisyah, didn't see our expression of anger and contempt.

Soon, we were back in adjacent cells at Tanglin.

29

Police Station Interrogation

After appearing in court, the cops wouldn't let me sleep. They left the light on in my cell. Guards checked to wake me up in case I fell asleep. I couldn't contact anyone, and nobody came to see me. Every day thereafter, we were interrogated in separate rooms.

The interrogation room had two chains suspended from the ceiling about 15 feet apart and two chains on the floor directly below. They hauled me out of bed early each morning for the next nine days, ordered me to strip to my shorts, and suspended me spreadeagled from the chains with wrist and ankle collars. I was getting thinner and paler, and now I was really tired. There was a spotlight on my private parts. Officer Lee entered the room and was seated at a table outside the spotlight. Officer Devanesan, who entered next, was hitting a bullwhip on a tabletop over and over. They were trying to get me to confess.

Officer Lee: "Are you sleepy, American asshole?"

"Yes, sir."

Lee: "Are you hungry for some nice juicy hamburgers? Let me hear you *beg*."

I said nothing. But I vividly recall everything.

Lee (to Devanesan): "Remove the blind from that window so this Jewboy can see what he's in for."

He then unveiled a window into another interrogation room, where Joey was completely naked, also tied up spreadeagled, while guards were ganging up on him, punching him, kicking his legs, spraypainting his private parts, and hitting him with traffic signs. I looked briefly, then turned my head away.

Lee (to Devanesan): "Move his head so he can see everything."

Devanesan moved my head so I might have a direct view of the beating, but I closed my eyes. (Actually, the scene was a tape of Joey's earlier torture, which prompted him to confess before our first court appearance.)

Lee: "Do you want that, white trash?"

"No, sir.'

Lee: "You have no choice in the matter, faggot. Confess you spraypainted those cars or you'll get the same, whiteboy!"

I said, "Did you get a video of me playing basketball that night?"

Lee: "The camera was turned off that night, whiteboy." Pushing a buzzer, "Let's see if this whiteboy can take it."

Devanesan then tore off my shorts. Next, eight Chinese police came into the room, including one policewoman. They put paper hats on my head with such words as "White Trash" and "American Asshole" and knocked them off, calling me "White trash" etc.

Lee: "Now, really give it to him."

For about the next two minutes, they hit me hard on the back, legs, and face with their fists until Officer Lee raised his hand for them to stop and they left.

Lee: "Confess! Admit you spraypainted those cars and we'll let you go. Otherwise, we'll continue."

"But I didn't do it. You've kept me here nine days and I've not confessed. Doesn't that prove my innocence?"

Lee: "Only a hardened criminal would hold out that long, you dumb whiteboy."

"But I've never been arrested before. I've never been in trouble."

Lee: "That was in America, where the law is lax. Here we convict you whether you're guilty or not, just to set an example to scare the rest."

"That's not true," I protested. "America has tough laws, but courts protect the accused from being treated like this. The American Embassy and my parents will get me out of here."

Lee: "We don't give a damn about your American Embassy. We don't give a damn about your parents. We don't give a damn about your country. They can't help you now. You're going to tell us what we want to hear."

While slapping my butt with the handle of the bullwhip, Devanesan gruffly intimidated me,

> "You need to be whipped on that white ass . . . to warm it up for the aircon room."

> "The aircon room? What's that?"

> Lee: "The aircon room is 35 degrees. We force you to squat and sit on a big block of ice. Your skin will no longer be white; it'll turn blue. We'll keep you there for hours until the ice slowly melts. If you try to move, we'll soak you with ice-cold water." Then, without realizing, he made a pun, "You'll be ai see, whiteboy."

("Ai see" means on thin ice, kind of what it sounds like—icy.)

> "Then what?" I asked.

> Lee: "Everyone confesses after our deep freeze torture . . . Now, we're going now for breakfast. I'm not listening to any more bullshit from you . . . When we come back, I expect you to confess or we'll take you to the aircon room, you piece of white crap. Bo pien."

(The latter phrase meant that I had no choice but to submit to what they wanted.) Both men left, slamming the door, leaving me chained.

At this point, I knew I couldn't last another full day of interrogation. The previous day, Joey told me in jail that they broke several of his ribs, so I feared more of the same for me. I only had 3 hours of sleep. So, I decided to confess. Later, I might retract the confession, saying I only confessed to stop the torture. The worst, I thought, was they could deport me back home to the USA.

The two officers returned.

> Lee: "Would you like some hamburgers for breakfast . . . or are you ready for the aircon room, white trash?"

> "OK, I admit to it. I'll sign a confession."

Lee nodded to Devanesan, who untied me and led me to sit at the table, where a typewritten paper and pen were ready. Devanesan then emptied my previously confiscated clothes, including a new pair of gym pants, from a black polyethylene bag onto the table.

> Lee: "Sign here . . . Then put on your clothes!"

I signed the goddamn paper without reading it and put on my clothes. Devanesan then led me to a police van outside the police station. I got into the van, driven by Aisyah, which went to Bukit Timah.

After signing the confession, they became nice to me. They drove me around various neighborhoods, asking me if I remembered spray-painting cars at various points along the road that they designated.

I told them what they wanted to hear. After that, they got me two hamburgers and drove me back to jail.

Within an hour or so, I was released from jail and entered a police car, which took me home. Devanesan rode with me in the back seat to watch me enter my apartment.

30

Back Home

After the police car approached the front door of the condo, I got out, accompanied by Devanesan Naroth. The doorman gave me a dirty look. We went into the elevator and up to the 30th floor where my parents seemed waiting for me. When the elevator door opened, Yan immediately hugged me. Devanesan left as soon as I entered our penthouse.

Dad, a bit distant:

> "We thought those road signs were just bought from a novelty store. Anyway, we got you good lawyers. You're home now. We support you fully, Jimmy."

Dad then called my attorneys to tell them I'd been released.

One of the attorneys—barristers, I mean—agreed to come over to our condo at the end of the day.

At about 5:30, before dinner, he rang us up from below, and Dad buzzed him in. After he entered our penthouse, he began to question me for details.

> Savundranayagam: "Did you admit to anything?"

"I signed a confession without reading it after nine days of torture. I even saw them torturing Joey."

Savundranayagam: "Well, then, we can ultimately plead guilty with extenuating circumstances. The next step is a court hearing Monday morning, when you can enter your new plea. In the meanwhile, I'll try for a plea bargain to lighten the sentence."

Dad: "Do you anticipate any difficulties in arranging that?"

Savundranayagam: "I'm not sure. The problem is that the government is cracking down on vandalism. According to news reports, cars have been damaged with hot tar, red spraypaint, eggs, bricks, and hatchets. Taxi drivers have complained that their tires have been slashed. Cars in some areas have been found with deep scratches and dents. A local judge found a line of red paint sprayed through the official seal on his car."

Addressing me, "Were you involved in this type of vandalism?"

"Well, I went with a group of guys from school on a few Sunday evenings. We just picked up discarded items from trash bins and along the roads. I'm told that, last Sunday, some of the guys went beyond that, but I never saw tar or anything like that. When the police asked me if I was engaged in vandalism last Sunday, I told them I was practicing basketball at the gym. The school had a surveillance camera, which must have taken pictures of me."

Savundranayagam: "I'll go to the school to get that tape. That'll be your ace in the hole."

Dad, relieved, said, "Thanks so much, Savundra." (He still couldn't pronounce the long name.) "I'm happy that my son is being represented by you. When should Jimmy report to the court again?"

Savundranayagam: "That depends. Ordinarily, trial would be set for next month. If I arrange a plea bargain with a fine and deportation sooner, I'll get Jim into court earlier."

"Good," said Dad, reassured.

"And thank you, too, Mr. Savundra," I said weakly. "I'll be ready. What's the fine if I lose?"

Savundranayagan: "I have no idea. In the thousands, perhaps."

Dad: "I'll pay whatever it is."

"Thanks, Dad," I said, still feeling bad.

Savundranayagan: "Call my office tomorrow afternoon. When I get a copy of the confession and the tape, we can plan from there."

Dad: "OK. Will do. Let's get this thing over so we can get back to normal!"

Then my barrister excused himself and left.

Yan and Dad hugged me again. I took a shower and tried to sleep, but I was too agitated and looked out the window most of the night from the chair in my room, now stripped of all the signs. I was so overwhelmed that my doctor prescribed Prozac until my trial.

I was too embarrassed to call Ling. Not yet hearing about my release, she didn't call either.

On an impulse, still troubled, I called Mom in Pennsylvania.

"Hi, Mom. How are you?"

Mom, happy to hear my voice: "How're *you* doing?" She obviously heard the news about me.

"Not so good, Mom. I got arrested for something I didn't do."

Disturbed, Mom said: "That's terrible. I'll get you a good Philadelphia lawyer to defend you."

"No need, Mom. Dad got a lawyer. He got me out of jail, and he'll be beside me in court."

Mom: "Well, just in case. You need the best lawyer you can get. I hear the Singland government isn't very nice in matters of the law."

"The lawyer here assures me everything will work out OK."

Mom: "I hope so. But the best lawyers in the world are in Philadelphia."

"I know, Mom."

"I love you, she said."

"I love you, too."

We then hung up.

31

Barristers' Office

Three days later, Dad, Yan, and I met at the office of my two barristers with an attorney who flew from Philadelphia on Mom's suggestion to help my case.

"Gentlemen," Dad said, "I want to introduce attorney Murray Rosen. Jimmy's mother in America has retained him, in case you allow him to join the case."

Bowing his head slightly toward the barristers, Rosen greeted them:

"Gentlemen!"

Savundranayagam: "We're pleased that you've come this distance to help organize our legal strategy."

Rosen shook hands with both barristers.

Suriyakumaran: "Based on his confession, James can be charged with up to 16 counts of vandalism. According to the law, the punishment for vandalism, where the graffiti leave indelible marks, is caning. Weird as it may seem, although the spraypaint has been removed, it's still up to the judge to decide whether spraypaint is considered indelible. The law prescribes 3 strokes of the cane for every count of vandalism, with a maximum of 24 lashes."

Yan: "That's 24 too many!"

Dad: "What's caning like?"

Savundranayagam: "You don't want James to be caned. The skin is split open, the pain is excruciating, and the marks leave permanent scars. However, no American has ever been caned in Singland before."

Suriyakumaran: "Less than 1 percent of all those convicted of vandalism are caned."

Yan: "That's still too many."

Dad: "Why do they use caning?"

Suriyakumaran: "In Singland, imprisonment is not considered punishment. For the most serious crimes, the government wants punishment. Severing the skin on someone's behind is a constant reminder not to repeat the same offense, or so they say."

Rosen: "How valid is the confession?"

Dad: "The confession was obtained through torture . . . Jim, read your statement."

"After I was freed," I began, opening an envelope with a typewritten paper, "I wrote the following: 'I would like to state that everything I told the police was a total lie because I was only scared of what they would do to me. They had physically and mentally hurt me."

Looking up from the paper, "I don't know truly who did the spraypainting. I, for sure, didn't do it."

Dad: "The doorman at our condo was questioned by the police, and he said that he didn't see Jim come home late with paint on his hands or clothes. The so-called confession just doesn't square with the facts."

Savundranayagan: "In Singland, a confession is a confession. The police deny they torture anyone to get a confession."

Suriyakumaran: "They don't have to charge James with all 23 counts. Instead, under the law, they could charge him with 4 counts of vandalism this year and jail him, 4 counts next year, and so on for the following years. Our best bet is a plea bargain. James pleads guilty to a lesser charge, pays a fine, goes to prison for a short time, but isn't caned."

Dad: "Is that likely?"

"Bruce, Eduardo, and Oliver told me yesterday," I interjected, "that they were formally charged with vandalism on Monday. They pleaded innocent and were released on bail. Bruce's father got a boat and took him out of the country, forfeiting bail rather than face possible caning. Eduardo and Oliver haven't been tried yet. I called Mom in Pennsylvania, and she thinks I'll get out of this mess faster if I just plead guilty, pay the fine, and do the jail time if it comes to that."

Yan: "Jim shouldn't be caned. This is barbaric. We don't do that in Taiwan."

Rosen: "I'll submit to the court two psychiatric reports from Philadelphia stating James suffers from symptoms of attention deficit hyperactivity disorder, a neurological ailment first diagnosed when he was 8, at the time of his parents' divorce, which accounts for his sometimes impulsive behavior. This should help to establish a case for mitigating circumstances— that he wasn't fully responsible for his actions."

Savundranayagam: "Good. We've been talking to the prosecutor's office. They've agreed that if James pleads guilty to 2 charges of malicious mischief for switching license plates and 1 of retaining the stolen property for the street signs, they'll drop the vandalism charges. Then he'll only have to pay a fine of $5,000 and serve up to 4 months in prison . . . And he won't be caned."

"I did pick up some street signs," I admitted, "so I may deserve some kind of punishment, but I don't want to be caned. If pleading guilty to a lesser charge will avoid caning, I'm for it."

Dad and Yan nodded "Yes."

I asked about Joey.

"What's going to happen to Joey Tan? He was accused of the same things."

Suriyakumaran: "He'll be tried soon, I hear. Maybe next month. We're not on that case."

Then all shook hands, and we left the office.

32

Media Frenzy

The next day, the newspaper *Straits Times* gave my arrest and pending trial more space than Joey's. They plastered pictures of the vandalism over the front and middle pages of the newspaper. Every day afterward, someone in the government made a comment. Letters to the editor, pro and con, were also printed. Those favoring my caning had Chinese names. Those opposing caning had European names or were from other Asian countries.

Ling called me later that day:

> "I'm sorry to hear what happened, but I'm glad you're out. Because the press will be all over us, we better not date for now. But I fully support you. The guys at school say Joey turned you in as a spraypainter. Please come back to school next Monday."

I didn't believe the gossip about Joey. He deserved my sympathy after all he had gone through. We were now in the same boat.

> "Thanks for your kind words, Ling," I said as calmly as I could. "I wondered why they kept picking on

me about the spraypainting. I wasn't even there that night."

We hung up with an exchange of "I love yous," starting with hers. I was so happy I had a friend who was sticking by me. I said to myself that I would marry her after this mess cleared up.

My arrest also made headlines in the *Philadelphia Inquirer* and the *New York Times*. Civil rights groups criticized the Singland government for being barbaric. Later, Dad showed me stories in the *New York Times*. One quoted Secretary of State Warren Christopher, who had been asked for a comment at a press conference.

> Christopher: "We have asked the Singland government to bring about justice in this case."

The U.S. Chamber of Commerce was also quoted:

> "We simply do not understand how the government can condone the permanent scarring of any 18-year-old boy— American or Singlander—by caning for such an offense."

In the same issue, the newspaper quoted Home Affairs Minister Henry Cheng:

> Cheng: "The United States can't tell *us* how to run our country. We are an independent country. We will bring about justice for the people of Singland. But we will not allow terrorists to run wild. We must provide an example of how we treat terrorists."

Meanwhile, leaders of right-wing organizations in the United States spoke out in favor of caning. Telephone calls to radio and television talk shows and letters to local newspapers and politicians favored caning as an answer to the supposed laxity toward juvenile delinquents and vandalism. It was as if the Singland government was in league with American right-wing groups.

I was counting on my lawyers to carry out what they promised. I had to wait five months before trial while the media hysteria continued and then quieted. I went back to school, but I stopped going to the gym. I focused on my studies instead and tried to keep to myself. Next semester, which was to begin in January, I decided not to continue with Chinese. My experiences make me angry with the Chinese, except Ling and Yan.

My former lunch table was occupied by other guys, so I ate with Eduardo and Oliver at a different table in the corner. Nobody wanted to eat with us. The two guys told me a lot of gossip about Joey—that he arranged for my initiation and he involved me in the so-called treasure hunt to get even with me for dating Ling. I stopped going to the disco on Fridays, but I continued dating Ling on Saturdays. I couldn't go out of the country on Sundays with Dad and Yan, as before, because the government held my passport.

At the end of December, during the holiday season when nobody noticed, Eduardo and Oliver pled guilty, were fined, and stayed in the country. Diplomatic pressure, I suppose, saved them. Joey's trial was still pending. So was mine.

My dates with Ling became increasingly passionate.

33

Next Court Appearance

Accompanied by my barristers, I went into court on a cloudy, drizzly morning. When I entered, the Court Bailiff escorted me to the Witness Box.

My two barristers sat at one table. At another table was a new prosecutor, Gerald Zhai.

Dad, Yan, Ling, and Warren from the American Embassy were in the gallery along with Vivian and about 20 teenage spectators from school.

Bailiff, as the Judge entered the courtroom:

"All rise."

Everyone stood and bowed slightly toward the Judge. Judge Arnold Kwok walked over to his seat and sat.

Court Bailiff: "You may be seated."

Everyone sat down but the Court Clerk, who announced,

"Case number 93125702. The People Versus James Alan Freeman."

Prosecutor Zhai, standing up,

"Your Honor, the defendant is charged 2 counts of malicious mischief for interchanging license plates, 1 of retaining stolen property for having street signs in his room at home, and 2 counts of vandalism for throwing an egg and a brick at 2 cars. We have decided not to charge him with the remaining original charges."

Judge: "How do you plead, Mr. Freeman?"

Savundranayagan: "Your Honor, we plead guilty to all five charges. We plead not guilty to the other charges."

Judge: "James Alan Freeman, this court finds you guilty of 2 counts of malicious mischief, 2 counts of vandalism, and 1 count of retaining stolen property. You are acquitted of the remaining charges."

Savundranayagan: "Your Honor, we petition for leniency. James is 18, an impressionable age, and he has attention deficit hyperactivity disorder, a neurological ailment that makes him prone to impulsive behavior. Ever since his parents divorced at an early age, his childhood was unhappy. This is his first offense. He has agreed to testify against any others who were arrested for the same offenses in future trials. We plead for a reduced sentence."

> Judge: "I will take the petition into account along with all the evidence in this case in determining the sentence." Banging the gavel, "Return to court on March 3 for sentencing."

We left the courtroom convinced that the sentence, in accordance with a plea bargain with the prosecutor, would be a monetary fine.

When we emerged, reporters asked us for a reaction to the sentence.

> Warren: "We see a large discrepancy between the offense and the punishment. The cars were not permanently damaged; brick and egg damage was easily fixed. Caning leaves permanent scars. In addition, the accused is a teenager and this is his first offense."

Warren had started a diplomatic row between Singland and Washington that would complicate the appeal for mercy.

Within hours of my conviction, I nevertheless felt extremely depressed. Dad took me to a hospital, where a psychiatrist examined me and gave me some medicine. I stayed home for the next few days before the next court date. Ling visited in the evenings to console me while we enjoyed Yan's delicious food.

Although I hadn't yet been sentenced, everyone at home was still confident that the worst was over.

But this was Singland.

34

The Sentence

Four days later, accompanied by my barristers, I went into court on a bright and sunny day. The Court Bailiff escorted me to the Witness Box.

At one table was prosecutor Gerald Zhai. My two barristers sat at an adjacent table.

Dad, Yan, Ling, and Warren were in the gallery along with Vivian and about 36 teenage spectators from school.

Bailiff, as the Judge entered the courtroom:

"All rise."

Everyone stood and bowed slightly toward the Judge. Judge Arnold Kwok walked over to his seat and sat down.

Court Bailiff: "You may be seated."

Everyone sat down but the Court Clerk, who announced,

"Case number 93125702. The People Versus James Alan Freeman."

Judge: "James Alan Freeman . . . you've committed several offenses that could not be condoned as a display of growing pains and schoolboy pranks . . . Although your counsel has asked for leniency, and you've offered to testify in future trials against those participating with you in committing these offenses, the law emphasizes the need to correct offenders so they'll not repeat . . . James Alan Freeman, you are hereby sentenced to a fine of $3,500 for having stolen property . . . 4 months in prison for malicious mischief . . . and . . . 6 strokes of the cane for vandalism."

He then banged his gavel.

Yan let out a wail. Dad hugged her. Ling and Vivian cried and hugged each other.

Grim-faced, I stood frozen.

Savundranayagan: "Your Honor, we believe that the sentence is entirely too severe. We plan to appeal the ruling."

Judge, banging the gavel: "Next case."

Obviously, those bastards doublecrossed us. But we went home, hopeful that the Chief Justice of the High Court would reduce the sentence on appeal.

35

Evening TV News

That same evening, Dad turned on the TV for news. Here's what we heard:

News Anchor Jill Eng: "A court today ordered James Freeman, an American teenager convicted of vandalizing cars, to be caned. For a comment from President Clinton, we take you to a press conference at the White House."

The camera then switched to the White House press corps room, with about 40 reporters seated.

David Donaldson: "President Clinton, an American 18-year-old has been sentenced in Singland to be caned for allegedly vandalizing cars. He claims he was tortured into making the confession on which the sentence was based. What's your comment on this situation?"

Clinton: "First I have heard of this. The sentence appears far too extreme. I'll look into it."

News Anchor Duncan Lau: "For a reaction from the American Embassy in Singland, we go to our correspondent, Sylvia Gomes."

Gomes: "I'm here at the steps of the American Embassy in Singland, talking to Chargé d'Affaires William Warren and James Freeman's American lawyer Murray Rosen." Addressing Warren, "What's the reaction of the American government to the court order to cane James Freeman?"

Warren: "The U.S. State Department has condemned caning as a human rights violation for years . . . In the case of James Freeman, we see a large discrepancy between the offense and the punishment. The cars weren't permanently damaged. The 'vandalism' was quite minor, whereas caning leaves permanent scars. Moreover, the accused is a teenager and this is his first offense."

Gomes: "Will the United States file a diplomatic protest?"

Warren: "The U.S. Embassy has informed the Singland government of our concerns regarding this case. We aren't going to forecast possible future diplomatic actions, but it's hard to imagine that U.S.-Singland relations would continue as if nothing much had happened if he's caned . . . In 1990, thousands of domestic workers from India and Thailand, because their visas had expired, were threatened with mass canings. When the two governments objected, Singland backed down . . . We plan to use as much pressure as we can to prevent James from being caned."

Gomes, addressing Rosen: "As James Freeman's lawyer, what's your reaction to the case?"

Rosen: "We're appealing the judge's decision to the High Court, and we're confident he'll reverse the sentence."

"Thank you, Chargé d'Affaires William Warren and attorney Murray Rosen. This is Sylvia Gomes, speaking from the steps of the American Embassy in Singland. Back to you, Duncan and Jill."

News Anchor Duncan Lau: "We now hear from our reporter Zach Kumar, who is standing by on the steps of the Ministry of Home Affairs with Minister Shiu-Feng Cheng."

Kumar (to Cheng): "Some Americans have made statements in opposition to the caning of Jim Freeman. What's your opinion on this matter, Minister Cheng?"

Cheng: "Our tough laws have kept our country orderly and relatively free of crime, unlike such cities as Chicago and New York, where even police cars are not spared the acts of vandals. We unreservedly support the decision of the judge."

Then after an interval of weather and sports news, the news anchor closed the broadcast.

Eng: "Thank you for listening. Stay tuned for late-breaking developments in the James Freeman case."

A theme song then ended the program.

While my barristers formulated an appeal on my behalf, I decided to stay home rather than return to school.

The court agreed to hear the appeal at the end of the month.

36

Appeal Denied

Four weeks later, I went to the High Court for a hearing on the appeal filed on my behalf. The room was much more elegant, with tapestries on the wall and velvet curtains over stained-glass windows. The atmosphere, however, was disrupted by very hard rain that morning.

My barristers led the way into court. When I appeared, the Court Bailiff escorted me to sit in the Witness Box.

My barristers sat opposite the table occupied by prosecutor Gerald Zhai and an assistant.

Dad, Yan, Ling, and Warren were in the gallery along with Vivian and nearly 70 spectators, consisting of some teenagers from school but almost outnumbered by radio and TV reporters.

Bailiff, as the Judge entered the courtroom:

"All rise."

Everyone stood and bowed slightly toward the Judge. Judge Shi-Hua Ping walked over to his seat and sat.

Court Bailiff: "You may be seated."

Everyone sat down but the Court Clerk, who announced,

"Case number 93125702. The People Versus James Alan Freeman."

All eyes and ears were then on the judge.

Ping: "On March 11, an appeal was filed regarding the sentence imposed by the Subordinate Court on March 3 regarding the case involving James Alan Freeman. This court has taken into consideration the various points raised in the appeal, the decision of Judge Arnold Kwok, and the facts in the case. The appeal points out that Mr. Freeman is young, has no criminal record, is remorseful about the vandalism to which he has confessed, and might be irrevocably harmed by the administration of caning as a punishment.

"The prosecution has responded that the basis for the conviction and sentencing is the Vandalism Act of 1966, which prescribes caning for vandalism with very little room for judicial discretion.

"Accordingly, I have deliberated for the past three weeks and come to the following conclusion: The purpose of the Vandalism Act is to deter vandalism with a sentence that is based on the extent of damage caused. In this case, vandalism did occur, relentlessly and willfully over a period of several days. Therefore, I cannot reverse the ruling of the Subordinate Court.

"James Alan Freeman, I affirm your sentence—a fine
of $3,500, 4 months in prison for malicious mischief,
and 6 strokes of the cane for vandalism. The appeal
is denied."

Immediately, the trap door opened behind me. Although I nearly fell
down, a Gurkha handcuffed me and escorted me down the ramp. A
police van awaited me. The Gurkha officer, named Rai, led me into
the van. The door closed. The van, operated by an older Malay man
named Mohammed, then drove to Queenstown Remand Prison.

I was now a prisoner of the government for the next four months, to
be caned at a date not yet designated. I felt that my life and future
had been raped.

The ruling was soon criticized on television by Chargé d'Affaires
Warren, I later learned. In response, an official of the government
lambasted him for his public statement, implying that he could have
filed a diplomatic protest instead. That may have been the beginning
of what was to come—a diplomatic row over the caning.

37

First Morning of Imprisonment

The police van stopped at Queenstown Remand Prison, a building powder blue and with cream trim. A police driver, Nathan Leong, escorted me to a check-in station. The police driver gave a file to Prison Clerk Todd Ng. A prison guard was standing by.

Prison Clerk Ng, looking at the file,

> "So *you* are James Freeman. Strip off, whiteboy."

> "Yes, sir."

When I kept my underwear on, Prison Clerk Ng emphasized,

> "*All* your clothes come off."

After I stripped completely, I was led into a room that appeared to be a doctor's office. Dr. Timothy Chen then examined my entire body as if I were taking a physical for the military.

I was then told to lie on top of a padded bench, used for examinations.

> Doctor: "We are now going to shave off all your hair."

I asked, "Why?"

Doctor: "Our prisoners come from everywhere. Some have body lice and could spread the lice to others. Body lice are very hard to eradicate and cause itching, especially for Caucasians, so we will put a cream on you after we shave you."

I then allowed the male prison nurse, Axle Liak, to shave my head, eyebrows, chest, armpits, legs, pubic area, and they turned me over to shave any hair on my back, back of my legs, and even from my balls and around my ass.

After that, they took me to a shower. After the shower, they took me back to the examining room and applied a cream where the hair was shaved off. Thank goodness for the cream, as I didn't itch afterward like in my initiation at school.

Then they issued me prison garments—a shirt with the name of the prison, short pants, flipflops, but no underwear.

"No underwear?" I asked as if they forgot something.

Nurse Liak: "It's too hot to wear underpants here. Especially with you, whiteboys, it would cause you jock itch."

I put the garments on, and Prison Guard Ng came in.

Prison Guard Ng, addressing Prison Guard Chow: "Take James Freeman to cell 446."

Prison Guard Chow, while escorting me to my cell: "So *you're* James Freeman. Welcome to Queenstown

Remand Prison. Behave yourself and you'll be well treated, whiteboy."

As he took me to my cell, I heard sounds from the other cells as if they were hitting the bars of the cell with something. Prisoners, as I passed their cell, called out

"Whiteboy. Whiteboy. Whiteboy . . ."

I didn't realize that my cellmate was eagerly waiting for me. He was doing pushups naked when Prison Guard Chow opened the cell door. As Prison Guard Chow closed the door, he got up. I saw an extraordinary 6-foot 200-pound Chinese body, with a shiny tanned complexion. He seemed a work of sculpture: All his muscles were big and well defined, especially his rounded pectorals, which stuck out at least 6 inches. He had well-defined, dense six-packs. Veins were popping out all over his arms. I had never seen such a body before, much better than the gymnasts at school. He had beautiful tattoos: One like a dragon on his back, the other an abstract design with waves, starting from his left shoulder and branching out toward his pectorals. As he faced me, I could see something change to an erect position, pointing up, not out. And it was very long. Nobody ever before showed such sexual excitement on seeing me, even Ling.

I'd heard about sex in American prisons, even rape in prison. But I knew little about such things before arriving in Singland. Now my worst fears were about to be confirmed—and in spades!

38

My Cellmate

When I entered my cell, my cellmate greeted me,

"So *you're* the famous James Freeman. Welcome to Queensway Remand. My name is Alexander Foong. But you should call me *Sir*."

I put my hand forward to shake his, saying,

"Pleasure to meet you, Alexander."

"Alexander what!" he demanded, raising his head upward, exposing his muscular neck, but not shaking my hand.

"Alexander Foong," I replied, as I lowered my hand. Evidently, he wasn't used to shaking hands when he met a new person.

"Wrong! Try again, whiteboy!"

"Alexander, Sir," I finally said.

"Just Sir," he emphasized.

"Sir," I said compliantly, wondering what I had gotten myself into.

"I'm 'Sir.' You're 'whiteboy.' Got it?"

"Yes, Sir."

"Louder, whiteboy."

"Yes, *Sir.*"

"That's right. You're learning good. You have a lot to learn, and I will be your teacher."

"My teacher, Sir?"

"Yes, your teacher. Everyone here knows you're going to be caned on your white ass. About half of the guys want to fuck that white ass."

I gasped.

He continued,

"So I will be your trainer—your Lim Peh." (By claiming to be Lim Peh, he was pretending to be my father or master in prison.) "I will prepare you so the caning will hurt as little as possible. I will show you some exercises to strengthen your butt. I will also protect you from the guys who want to fuck you. But you have to obey *me*. You have to do whatever I say. I have my own sexual needs, and you will satisfy them whenever I want. But don't worry, I don't have a big sex appetite." (That proved to be an understatement!)

On the outside, I like girls. Now, what do you think of that, whiteboy?"

"I'm grateful if you can prepare me for the caning. But I'm straight. I don't have sex with guys."

"When you talk to me, always end your sentences with the word *Sir*! Got it?"

"Yes, *Sir*," I uttered, almost mumbling.

Alex: "Straight or gay. It doesn't matter here. We Chinese have sex with both. We fuck the girls to show our superiority over the weaker sex. We have sex with guys to have fun. We aren't stupid Americans, whiteboy, throwing away our chances for good sex."

"I won't enjoy it, *Sir*."

Alex: "Enjoy? It doesn't matter whether *you* enjoy it or not. While you're in this cell, your job is to give *me* enjoyment. Got it, whiteboy?"

I didn't know what to say, so I nodded. He looked mad, so I said,

"Yes, *Sir*."

He then smiled, as if pleased that I would be very obedient.

"How do you know about me, *Sir*?" I asked.

Alex, pointing to the TV in his cell, "You've been on TV, whiteboy. Everyone's been talking about you. You're the first American ever sentenced to be caned in Singland."

"My lawyers are appealing for clemency to the President of Singland, Sir."

"Don't count on it. The government wants to show that it's tough. They love to show no mercy."

"What's it like to be caned, Sir?"

Pointing to the next cell, "See that Chinese guy lying naked on his side in the cell over there?" To the Chinese guy, "Say, Chong, show the whiteboy your ass."

Chong stood up and bent over, revealing eight deep scars, almost evenly spaced, on a bright reddish- purple posterior.

Chong: "Kiss it, whiteboy!"

Alex: "Up yours, purple ass!"

Explaining to me, "Chong was caned last week. Since then, it's been too painful for him to sit, so he lies on his side . . . When he eats in the mess hall, he squats over the bench, pretending to sit down, so the guards won't punish him for refusing to sit according to regulations . . . The worst is when he has to shit, he usually screams. As the shit travels past the scar outside his ass, it moves slowly and irritates the wound."

I then said,

"That's inhuman."

Alexander: "No. That's Singland."

He began laughing defiantly at the government, and I joined in. The laughter helped me to relax and gave me more respect for him. Maybe, I hoped, he was a decent guy despite his sexual habits. But then . . .

39

Enslavement

Before I had a chance to catch my breath, Alex ordered, "Now strip for inspection, whiteboy! Chop-chop! I want to see the ass that's going to be caned. I need to know how much work you'll have to do to build the muscles to be ready for that cane."

As I took off my prison clothes, he pointed to an empty hook in the wall alongside other prison clothes, so I put my top and bottom clothes there.

When I was completely naked, he examined my body, feeling me all over—my shoulders, pectorals, biceps, waist, back, thighs, and finally grabbed and massaged my butt. Then he spanked me very hard.

> "Very soft, whiteboy. You've got a lot of work to do to build up that ass. You're lucky to have me as your trainer. When we use the weights in the prison yard, I'll train you to get some muscles in those flabby butts." Then he spanked me hard again.

"Thank you, Sir."

I was grateful. I didn't think my butt was *that* soft until he spanked me.

Then he turned to one side and ordered,

> "Feel my butt, whiteboy! See how Chinese build up their butts! We have to. Our parents cane us when we're growing up, so we go out for gymnastics and build our bodies while you guys in the West allow yourselves to have faggot bodies."

I felt his right butt, then his left butt. He was right. They were smooth but hard as a rock. Shaped like bubbles. I congratulated him,

> "Wow! You really have a hard butt. Like a rock!"

He glared at me. Then I remembered to say, "Sir."

> "That's good, whiteboy. Now bend over and grab your ankles."

At first, I said "Huh!" very softly, but I complied when I saw the fierce look on his face.

I am embarrassed to tell you what happened next. Please don't judge me. I just have to get it off my chest—my pectorals, if you like. I am only writing this so you, the reader, will understand what I went through and why my life changed so much after I got out.

Here's what he said next:

> "Now spread that ass, whiteboy! Chop-chop!"

I grabbed both cheeks and pulled them away, exposing my asshole.

"A virgin! Wow! You weren't lying. It'll be a pleasure
to be your first!"

I realized that he planned to fuck me. How could I resist him? He
was *much* stronger than me. But I said nothing, pulled my hands
away, and started to stand up.

"Who told you to stand up, whiteboy?"

"Nobody . . . Sir." I realized he was a disciplinarian.

"From now on, you will obey me, whiteboy. Or get
punished. Get it?"

"Yes, Sir."

"You want me to pang jio you, whiteboy? Or pang
sai you?"

"No, *Sir!*"

He was threatening to piss or shit on me as punishment.

"Now stand up, whiteboy. Turn around."

Then he performed a kung fu move. I was suddenly on the floor. His
body was on top of mine, with his right elbow digging into my neck,
and his cock pointing directly at my mouth.

His cock, hard ever since I entered the cell, was at least seven inches,
I think. Thick. I could see veins in his hard cock, sticking out like
the veins in his arms.

"Now I'm going to test you, whiteboy: Suck!"

Then he glared at me as if to say, "Do it or else!"

Totally astonished, I started slowly to put his smooth cock in my mouth, just like when I saw Eiji suck Joey.

"Suck it, whiteboy."

I had no choice. I had to suck him. I opened my mouth and slowly put my lips on the tip, then moved toward his balls. He had little pubic hair.

"Enjoy it, whiteboy! No teeth!"

My jaw muscles strained, and I began to suck like a baby.

"Corright. You doing good, whiteboy!"

("Corright" is Singlish for correct.)

I wondered how long it would take, but he came fast. I didn't want to swallow, but a lot of juice came out. It tasted kinda sweet.

"Swallow it, whiteboy! Very slowly! All of it! That's a good boy."

Then he caressed and patted my newly shaved head as if I really were a little boy.

"Now thank Sir," he ordered gently.

"Thank you, Sir," I repeated.

He got off my body and ordered me to get up.

Now I wondered how often I would have to service him. He seemed very sex-oriented, and his body was fantastic. Women would fight to have a chance for his body. But now he had no women. He only had me. But I wasn't a woman, and I didn't intend to become gay. Besides, he was going to train me to withstand caning. So, he wanted me to be strong, not some girly faggot.

Alex: "While you're in this cell, you're to be naked at all times, ready to obey and please me, whiteboy. I will do the arrowing." (Singlish for ordering). "Only put your prison shorts on when we go to meals. Always sit with me at the mess table, with your head looking down, so the other guys'll know you're mine. Otherwise, they might try to rape you. But if they try, I'll threaten them, and nobody here *ever* challenges me. You're lucky to have me. Isn't that right, whiteboy?"

"Yes, Sir," I said almost mechanically.

"You want them to fuck you, whiteboy?"

"No, Sir."

"You know I can get the Gurkha guards to come in and dominate you. You want that, whiteboy?"

"No, Sir."

(Some of the Gurkhas were hideous in appearance.)

"Then from now on, your ass is mine. My property. Exclusively. If you try to disobey, I will turn you loose, and they will gang rape you. Understood, whiteboy?"

"Yes, sir."

In other words, he wanted me his slave. But at least, he would take care of me.

"Now you take the bottom bed. I'll sleep on top. Remember that! I'm the top guy. You're the bottom boy. Say it, whiteboy!"

"You are the top guy," I parroted. "I'm the bottom boy. *Sir.*"

"Good. You're learning fast, whiteboy."

He then snapped his fingers and pointed to the bottom of the bunk bed. I crawled in, though I was very much awake. He continued to stand outside my bed, showing off his muscles.

After a few minutes, I spoke softly,

"May I ask what you're in for, *Sir*?"

"Yes, whiteboy. I was convicted of rape. The ger I supposedly raped wanted sex with me. But her father, a minister in the government, was outraged that I fucked her and made her pregnant. To prevent our getting married, he arranged to put me in prison until she would get married to someone *he* wanted. She has terrific neh neh pok (big boobs) and visits me from time to time and has held out to be my bride. But as long as she does, I'm locked up here."

"Sorry to hear that," I said. Then I remembered, "Sir."

He seemed very straightforward. And his cell was well equipped. He had a TV, comfortable mattresses, and clean sheets. He had a chair, a desk, and some magazines—bodybuilding magazines. From what I saw as I passed the other cells, his cell was the best. He had somehow impressed the prison management. I didn't realize that he was a famous bodybuilder. That's why he got such good treatment. And, I figured, he chose me as his cellmate so he could boast that he had a white slaveboy.

40

Prison Mess Hall

As I heard a bell ring, the cell door opened as if set on a timer. He spanked my ass again and said,

"Time to get ready for lunch, whiteboy!"

"Yes, Sir."

Pointing to his prison clothes, he snapped his fingers.

I then brought him his pants. He snapped his fingers again and motioned that I was to help him put his pants on, so I did. I then put mine on, too.

I next followed close behind Alex to the prison mess hall, set up like a cafeteria.

When we walked down the stairs into the room, I gazed into a sea of muscular ah bengs (tough guys), wearing only pants. Not all were Chinese. I saw a lot of Malays, some Tamils, and two or three Caucasians. The Chinese seemed to have the best physiques. Alex guided me to the bench where he always sat. He pointed next to him and snapped his fingers, so I sat down where he wanted me and looked down, not at the others around the table. There were about eight of them.

"This is James Freeman," he announced to his friends. "He has agreed to be my property. Don't even touch him with a handshake. You know the consequences."

The Chinese appeared to nod.

One (Yen) said, "Good. We're happy you've made a new conquest—a whiteboy. If you need us to discipline the whiteboy, we're here to help. Anytime. Out of respect for you, Alex. We liked it when you let us have fun with your last disobedient whiteboy!"

Another one (Lim) said, "What are you going to do with him, Alex?"

Alex then told them, "I'm going to train him to toughen up his butt for the caning. Some training will take place with the weights in the yard. Some will be when we're in the cell together. He's already given me good service, and there's more to come."

(I think he meant "cum.")

A third guy (Chiang) said, "You sure know how to train them, Alex. More power to you. And this time you're lucky—you've got a goondu whiteboy. We'll see more when we shower for the night! Ha! Ha!"

("Goondu" means "idiot.)

Shower for the night? That seemed rather odd

A fourth guy (Yap) asked, "What do you have to say for yourself, whiteboy?"

Keeping my head down, I whispered,

"I'll be loyal to Sir."

"Sir!" said a fifth (Wong) voice. "Wow, Alex! You've already trained him good. I'll be happy to tekan him when you get out of here. Whenever that is!"

("Tekan" refers to being a bully. He lusted for me, I guess.)

Alex: "Don't zi siao the whiteboy anymore. He's mine and that's that."

(In other words, he wanted to stop them from teasing me and was warning that he could serve up his own reprisal.)

The food was now out, and tables were being called by number. Our table was #1, so we were called first. Alex was first in line. I was second. Whoever was third in line stroked my butt softly when Alex wasn't looking. I figured they all wanted to fuck me if they ever got the chance.

The helpers filled out plates with fish, spinach, and rice with some kind of hot sauce. Alex sat back down first and snapped his fingers while pointing to where I should sit (in the same place as before). We sat down and ate our Chinese food. Not as good as restaurant food, of course, but not bad if you like Chinese food.

When we finished, Alex got up to take the tray back to the conveyer belt, snapped his fingers at me so I would follow, and then led me on the way back to the cell.

When we got back to the cell, he closed the door and stripped naked. I followed.

> Alex: "You were a good boy with the guys, whiteboy. But don't pay any attention to them. They all want to fuck you, but I won't allow that. You're safe with me."

> "Thank you, Sir" was all I could say.

41

TV News Broadcast

My cellmate Alex had a television set in his room and liked to watch news and sports after the evening meal. This night was no exception.

News Anchor Jill Eng: "James Freeman's appeal to revoke his caning sentence was rejected by the High Court today. His lawyers are now pursuing the final avenue of appeal—a request for a pardon from Singland President Fu Kwang Chu."

News Anchor Gordon Lau: "We have in our studio one of the barristers who sought the appeal. Mr. Suriyakumaran, what were the grounds for the appeal?"

Suriyakumaran: "We argued that caning was inappropriate because Jim Freeman would be left with *permanent* marks on his body, but he was only accused of vandalism, and the damage from bricks and eggs was easily fixed. Moreover, no eyewitness saw him engage in vandalism. There was only his confession, which was elicited under duress while he was threatened during police interrogation."

Lau: "Thank you, barrister Suriyakumaran . . . For the view of the government, Julia Wing Lim is standing by with Home Affairs Minister Shiu-Feng Cheng outside the ministry building."

Lim: "Home Affairs Minister Cheng, caning will leave permanent scars on Jim Freeman's body, but the damage has already been reversed. Why, his barrister asks, support such a harsh punishment?"

Cheng: "The American boy freely admitted that he engaged in vandalism. According to the law, vandalism is punishable by caning. Courts have already caned thousands of persons for the same offense. So we cannot make an exception in this case. Justice must be impartially applied to all."

Lim: "This is Julia Wing Lim at the Ministry of Home Affairs. Back to you, Gordon and Jill."

Lau: "There was a reaction from President Clinton at today's White House press conference."

Next, the picture changed to a White House press conference, with about 30 journalists present.

American journalist Helene Thomasini: "President Clinton, yesterday Singland's Chief Justice turned down your appeal for clemency for American teenager James Freeman. Are you surprised that he wasn't freed?"

Clinton: "I've not objected to the young man being punished. I've not objected to the young man being incarcerated. I've objected to this caning. As a result, James Freeman is going to bleed considerably and may have permanent scars. I think it's a mistake."

American journalist Sam Broder: "Mr. President, a *New York Times* editorial urges American companies with Singland subsidiaries to press the Singland government to back down on the caning of James Freeman. What's your opinion?"

Clinton: "I'm undecided about whether to call on U.S. corporations doing business in Singland to pressure the government."

American journalist David Huntley: "Mr. President, former President George Bush will be visiting Singland in two weeks to give an Asian Leadership lecture. What should he say to the government when he arrives?"

Clinton: "President Bush will have to decide for himself what he wishes to say. But if he decides to say something in opposition to the caning, I would certainly be grateful for that."

News Anchor Gordon Lau: "Singland TV has just learned that 24 United States Senators have signed a petition asking President Fu Kwang Chu of Singland to commute the sentence of James Freeman so that he won't be caned . . . We now take you to outside Singland's parliament, where our correspondent Sylvia Gomes is standing by with Maine Senator William Cohen, who hasn't signed the petition."

Gomes: "I'm here with American Senator William Cohen, who has just emerged from a meeting with Deputy Prime Minister Low Heng Tao and Senior Minister Low Chai Liang . . . Senator Cohen, what are the odds that President Fu will grant clemency to James Freeman?"

Cohen: "I gathered from the leadership that they're not going to yield. They resent the West telling them what they should do and they're obviously ready to take the consequences. It has become a test of wills. Will Singland yield to pressure from the US? The answer is no. But I do not foresee any disruption in political relations between the US and Singland."

Gomes: "This is Sylvia Gomes. Back to you, Gordon and Jill."

News Anchor Eng: "For a reaction directly from the American Congress, we take you to Capitol Hill, where our reporter Sarita Shou is in the office of Congressman Tony Hall, who represents James Freeman's district."

Shou: "I'm here with Kenneth Fowler, spokesman for Representative Hall. Mr. Fowler, what's Congressman Hall's position on the James Freeman case?"

Fowler: "Tony Hall strongly supports the effort to seek clemency for James Freeman.

Shou: "What about people in your district? Have they written Congressman Hall on the case?"

Fowler: "As a matter of fact, we've received many letters. Most actually oppose the Congressman's efforts. However, the Congressman believes that the writers of the letters don't understand the enormous severity and cruelty of the punishment."

"This is Sarita Shou at the office of Representative Tony Hall in Washington. Back to you, Gordon and Jill."

Lau: "For another view, our reporter Duncan Soong is standing by at Harvard University with Political Science Professor Charles Adams Berton, an expert on Singland."

Soong: "Why, in your opinion Professor Berton, has Singland decided to cane James Freeman?"

Berton: "Beneath the surface, Singland's action exposes a continuing sense of cultural superiority that some Asians, Chinese in particular, feel to many foreign nations, especially America . . . Most of those who want James Freeman caned are just venting their frustration over our American criminal justice system."

Soon: "This is Duncan Soong at Harvard University. Back to you, Gordon and Jill, in Singland."

Eng: "We now hear from Prime Minister Ho Mang Chin, who is outside the steps of parliament with our reporter, Sarita Shou."

Sarita Shou: "Prime Minister Ho Mang Chin, there has been a lot of criticism of the Singland government from leaders in America. What is your assessment of the situation?"

Ho: "The U.S. government, the U.S. Senate, and the U.S. media took the opportunity to ridicule us, saying the sentence was too severe. But the United States does not restrain or punish individuals consistently. Sometimes criminals are even forgiven for whatever they have done. That's why the whole country is in chaos—drugs, violence, unemployment, and homelessness. The American society is the richest and most prosperous in the world but it is hardly safe and peaceful. You know that if you come to Singland, your life, limb, and properties will be quite safe."

"But not your ass," I ejaculated, causing my cellmate to laugh.

Alex, quickly turning the TV to sports:

"You're popular, whiteboy. The president of the United States is thinking about you. But you and I know you *will* be caned. And you need my help so it won't hurt."

"Yes, *Sir*" was the only thing that I could think to say.

Once again, the broadcast demoralized me. The same type of news continued Thursday and Friday night.

Dad taped all these news programs so that I could view them again in case I wanted to write a book on my ordeal. Now I am, and reliving the past may be a way to achieve a catharsis over the trauma to my consciousness. But such memories are still extremely painful.

42

Shower

At 9 p.m., on my first day in prison, there was a ringing sound in our part of the prison.

Alex: "It's time to shower, whiteboy. Follow me."

"Shower?" I asked. "Why now, Sir?"

"Stupid whiteboy! We wash off our skin before going to bed every night so we'll not soil the prison sheets on our bed. Don't you Americans do that, whiteboy?"

"No, Sir. We just shower in the morning."

"How backward you Americans are! Don't you *ever* think of being sanitary? We shower in the morning, too, whiteboy."

Then he opened the cell door and went out. I followed behind. There was a long line of naked bodies walking to the shower on the floor below. When we got to the shower room, water was already on. Alex snapped his finger and pointed to the farthest end of the shower. Then he started showering next to me. I faced the shower and didn't look at anyone, though I felt that all eyes were focused on me, especially my ass.

When the water stopped, the guys filed out to the drying room. Prison workers issued us fresh towels. Alex got two and handed one to me. Then he went to one side of the room, pointed to the corner, and tried to snap his wet fingers. I went where he pointed. While drying off our wet bodies, I again marveled at his impressively muscular body, but I didn't look beyond. I knew the other guys were gazing at me, but I was afraid to look at them. When Alex finished, he folded up his towel, went to the exit, deposited his towel in the discard bin, and I followed, copying his every move. Then he went back to the cell, and I followed.

This time, however, those in the other cells could see me, front and back.

As we passed, I could hear them say:

> "Nice body for a whiteboy!"

> "Wrong. All whiteboys have ugly bodies!"

> "Get a load of that white ass! It'll be purple soon!"

> "Not such a big one! Americans always boast they're bigger than us. But they're not."

> "That Alex is a lucky guy! He's training that whiteboy good!"

Yes, I was thoroughly humiliated that day. Alex was taking care of me like a father. But also like a sex maniac. I guess I was lucky to have him. I looked forward to building the muscles in my butt.

We went into the cell. He closed the door, immediately snapped his fingers, and pointed to his cock, which was hard again. I then got down on my knees to do my duty. He ordered me to jack off while sucking him. In other words, there was some enjoyment for me while he was the main beneficiary. Yes, I was getting used to being his sex slave. But I still didn't like it.

Afterward, he snapped his fingers and pointed to the bottom of the bunk bed. I got in. After reading a few magazines for about 15 minutes, he got in his own bed. It was already dark outside. Singland's at the equator, after all. After the lights went out at 10 p.m., we slept fairly soundly until morning.

43

First Workout

A buzzer went off at 6 the following morning. Alex had already gotten out of bed and was sitting in his chair. I jumped out next to him, still a bit sleepy.

"Did you sleep well, whiteboy?"

"OK." He glared, and I realized that I had to say "Sir!"

"Time for your morning duty, whiteboy!" I knelt down before him and complied.

"We shower now, whiteboy. Same as before."

We repeated the same routine as the previous night, though those in the adjacent cells didn't comment with words. Instead, they made sucking sounds as I went by, including Chong, who was still lying on his side.

After shower came breakfast. Same routine. One of the Chinese guys felt my right leg and reached for my cock under the table, but I said nothing. While in line for the food, someone poked into my ass, and again, I decided not to tell Alex. I didn't want to cause trouble.

The Chinese breakfast of congee (boiled soupy rice with soy sauce) wasn't bad. Not good either. As time went on, I got bored with the same breakfast day after day.

Back to the cell, Alex had something in mind: At about 10:00, he ordered me to put on my pants and led me to the gym. We were the first ones there. It was outside, consisting of benches, barbells, and weights. Soon, there were about 20 muscular guys going through their routines with partners. I was Alex's partner.

> "Spot me, whiteboy," he ordered, as he lied on one of the benches and started to push about 80 kilograms. (Close to 180 pounds.) Benchpress, they call it.

> "What, sir?"

> "To 'spot' means to check if I lift too much. If I struggle, help me get the pole back to the rack."

> "OK, Sir. Will do, Sir."

As he benchpressed, I could see his enormous pectorals strain to the max. When he finished three times (three sets), he asked me to lie on the bench. He put only 10 kilos on the pole, 5 on each side, and I easily pushed that.

> "Good boy," he said, praising me.

Then he increased the weight to 20 kilos, and my third set was for 30 kilos, but he had to spot the third set, as I wasn't used to lifting weights and couldn't complete that set.

Afterward, he led me to a place where barbells were lying on the ground with small weights on either end. He picked two up very carefully, held them up on both sides, close to his pectorals, then stood with his feet apart and bent his knees, lowering them into a squat, and then stood up.

"That's a squat," he said. "Now your turn, whiteboy."

He gave me the barbells, both with 10- kilogram weights, 5 on each, and said,

"Squat, whiteboy."

As I lowered my body, he checked to see that my torso was upright throughout.

"Good, whiteboy!" he encouraged.

After that, the barbell weights went up to 15 and 20.

"Do you feel your butt while you do that?" he asked.

"Yes, *Sir*!"

"That's the first exercise to strengthen your butt, whiteboy. Here's the second—the lunge."

He showed me how, and I copied him.

After that, he showed me various types of lunges, then the one-legged deadlift, and the hip extension. My butt got sore fast, and I made sounds of pain.

"Focus your mind on your butt. Think about the muscles in the butt and how you are giving them more blood. Like a massage."

"That's the way I feel, Sir!"

During my time at the gym, I kept hearing loud screams.

"What're those noises, Sir?" I asked Alex.

"Some of those who are caned make a lot of noise,
don't they," he replied.

While I did more sets of my butt exercises, he did all sorts of lifting—heavyweights. Back, shoulders, arms. Sit-ups with weights. He exercised his whole body, while I just focused on my butt. We seemingly drank gallons of water as we perspired under the clouded sky.

In the coming weeks, I alternated exercising my butt on one day, then the rest of my body on the other days. At least my body might be more spectacular when I left, even if my butt got lacerated by the cane. The sound of the screams, which I heard from time to time after that, gave me more incentive to work on my butt.

Afterward, we went to the shower. We removed our shorts and showered. Then we went back to our cell. Soon, it was time for lunch. As we walked out of the cafeteria, he let me go first and ordered me to run up the steps—also a butt exercise, he said.

44

A Very Different Butt Exercise

When we got back to the cell after lunch, I crashed. I was really tired, and my muscles began to ache, typical of the soreness resulting from a first workout.

At about 5, I woke up to see him looking out the window. Then he started doing pushups. Soon I was to learn a new exercise. Or was it an exercise?

> "Come here, whiteboy!"

I climbed out of the bunk bed, while he pointed to the floor. I thought he was going to order me to do pushups, and he did.

> "Do 50 pushups, whiteboy!"

I did 20 quite fast, then slowed down and stopped after 25 and just lay down on the floor. Then he came on top of me, put some kind of cream in my ass, put his hands over mine so I couldn't move, and he slowly plunged into me.

> "Ouch, Sir!" I said. I just knew that he would eventually penetrate me, and it hurt as I resisted the intrusion.

"This is another butt exercise, whiteboy. The aim is for me to slam against your ass as hard as possible. Instead of a cane, you feel the weight of my body, whiteboy. It toughens your gluteus maximus."

"I see, Sir!"

As I gave a sign of pain, he said,

"Don't fight it, whiteboy. It hurts less when you relax and don't try to block it."

He was right, I gradually learned. I even found that there was an odd sort of pleasure as he moved in and out. Fortunately, he exploded very quickly, so the agony was short.

"This is what the guys want to do to you, whiteboy. They do it to women on the outside. But they will show no mercy to you, and they might even cause bleeding. Now, to let the stress out, I want to hear you say "I submit,' whiteboy!"

"I submit, *Sir.*"

"Again!"

"I submit, *Sir.*"

"Good. Say that whenever I do this to you again."

Then I could feel him release me from his grip.

"Now say, 'Thank you!"

"Thank you, *Sir.*"

He was obviously brainwashing me. I didn't really believe it would help my butt. But I knew he would eventually do it to me sometime. At least he wasn't gay. And neither was I. He was relieving sexual frustration, but at my expense.

I had a choice—submit to him or get raped by many prisoners. And I made my choice. He had the power. I befriended and pleased that power, so it made me feel a little powerful as well. In the process, I was becoming like the good citizens of Singland in accepting a government that could, if disobeyed, become very ruthless.

Anyway, what developed was a daily routine—wake up, suck, shower, breakfast, gym, shower, lunch, nap, pushups and you know what. Next, the daily routine was the evening meal, TV, shower, and sleep. It was difficult to follow the routine at first, though he was not always hungry for me. I could not keep up with his energy level at all. Nevertheless, the regularity of it all made me feel less apprehensive that he would do something unexpected.

45

First Prison Visit

After the same routine on Saturday morning, it was the one day each week for an outside visitor. A security guard summoned me to appear at a visitor window at 3. Alex also had a visitor at that time. We put on our clothes, and he escorted me there.

Dad, Yan, and Ling were there to greet me. I asked permission to deliver a written note to Ling, but the security guard took it from me as I entered the room. Not allowed to touch or hug, we looked at each other through the window and talked by telephone.

Dad: "How're they treating you, son?"

"Not bad. My cellmate is showing me how to strengthen my ass for the caning."

Dad: "We're working on that. Washington is trying to stop the caning."

"I hope so, Dad," I purred. "Meanwhile, I'm getting stronger."

Yan: "Who's your cellmate, Jim?"

(I was no longer "Jimmy." Now I was "Jim.")

"Alex Foong," I said proudly. I then pointed to him in another part of the visitor room.

Ling: "Alexander Foong! Wow! He's the top bodybuilder in Singland. You're lucky to have him as your teacher, Jim!"

Yan interjected: "That girl over there, talking to him, is Elizabeth Hee, daughter of the Deputy Minister of Labor."

Ling: "Yes, when I walk over past the prison, which isn't far from where I live, I see her standing about 5, looking toward one of the windows. I realize now that's where you are, too, Jim."

I then exclaimed, "So that's why he keeps looking out of the window! Now I know his girl really misses him, and he longs for her very much."

Ling: "From now on, I'll try to stand with her. Maybe I can make a new friend, Jim."

Dad: "Well, prison doesn't sound that bad, son. But we're doing everything to get you out without any caning."

"Thanks, Dad. I need the encouragement after seeing Singland TV on my case."

Dad: "I know. They slant the news. We get the *New York Times* at work, and most stories focus on caning as a serious human rights violation. Editorials demand that Clinton do something to get you released."

"Meanwhile, Dad, I'm getting ready for that day, just in case."

Dad: "Jim, what do you want me to tell your Mom in Pennsylvania?"

I said, "Tell her to keep praying for me, I love everyone, and I'm keeping strong inside and outside my body."

Ling: "We all love you, Jim, and we'll stand by you."

"Thanks. I really appreciate your love and support. All of you."

Time was up. We said goodbye, and a guard returned me to my cell. Alex was already back in our cell.

Entering our cell,

"Now I know why you look out the window at 5 each day, Sir." (I wanted to be friendly.)

"Oh, you found out about that, whiteboy. Yes, I have a special admirer."

"So do I, Sir. My girlfriend will try to join yours from now on."

"That's good, whiteboy. I bet your girl would choose me if she could."

"Not a chance, Sir. My girl loves me. When I get out, I'll ask her to marry and take her home to the USA."

"Don't be too sure about it, whiteboy. Chinese girls are sometimes pressured to do something their family wants. Have you met them?"

"No. We've been dating . . ."

"Bad sign, whiteboy. If you meet the parents, and they like you, your plans will work. But now that you're in prison, they might shun you, whiteboy."

I said nothing, stunned that I might never marry Ling, the one person who might fulfill my dream to marry, go to college, and have kids after starting a good high-paying job.

After that, joined by Alex, I saw Ling and Elizabeth on the walkway outside the prison every day at 5. While we gazed together, he often became hard and ordered me to service him. I had become used to that by now, though I hated it. Fortunately, he tended to explode very fast.

46

TV News from the United States

The next day, I had to service him at the usual time in the morning and let him top me after we gazed at our girlfriends at 5. After he fucked me, he usually ordered me to jack off. That way, I kinda looked forward to submitting to his big appetite.

But if I didn't cum soon, he might ask me to stand up and lick his enormous pectorals while jacking off. They were rounded and hard, like giant cushions, and the skin was very smooth. They were much bigger than the boobs of the Chinese girls. I could tell he enjoyed having them licked. It was almost like kissing him. At first, he would tell me to stop if I didn't cum, but as time went on, the cum seemed to flow almost automatically as I worshipped his body.

The evening news focused on me again:

> News Anchor Gordon Lau: "Regarding the case of James Freeman, who has been sentenced to be caned in Singland, former President George Bush made a statement yesterday while addressing 200 officials and diplomats at a luncheon here."

George Herbert Walker Bush: "I can remember being spanked as a child, and it did me good . . . Although caning is brutal, I doubt that an American offender should be punished differently from a citizen of Singland for the same crime . . . We don't have caning as a punishment in the United States, and I am certainly not advocating that system for the United States, but I think of the Singland work ethic, I think of democracy, I think of prosperity, and I think of safe streets. You Singlanders have much to teach us."

Lau: "What Bush may have said behind the scenes in meetings with government leaders wasn't clear, but his remarks have been interpreted as a go-ahead to cane James Freeman."

Then there were quick-burst news quotes from the United States:

Senator William Bennett: "The American people believe too many people are getting away with serious crimes and not paying any kind of price."

Sacramento City Council Representative George Kentowsky: "I've introduced a bill in the City Council to have caning for vandalism in Sacramento. We're sick and tired of graffiti."

Philadelphia City Council Representative Walter Wilson: "James Freeman used to live here in metro Philadelphia. If he ever does the same thing here, I want him caned, so I'm introducing a bill in the City Council to have caning for any juvenile found guilty of a felony."

News Anchor Jill Eng: "A Newsweek poll shows 38 percent of Americans favor the caning of James Freeman. A Time/CNN poll reports 46 percent approval of the caning sentence of James Freeman. A Los Angeles Times poll found 49 percent approval of James Freeman's caning sentence." For the opinion of a member of Congress, I now transfer to Margaret Leong in Washington.

Leong: "I'm in the office of California Congressman Dan Kerkvliet. What's your opinion about the caning of American James Freeman?"

Kerkvliet, in a Congressional office with 20 paddles of different kinds on the wall: "I've introduced a bill in Congress to have paddling as punishment for any drug-related offense. That'll stop the drug trafficking for sure."

"Back to you, Gordon and Jill."

Eng: "Another reporter, Margaret Leong, is standing in Washington with one of the Senators who signed the petition to have James Freeman's sentence commuted."

Leong: "I'm here in the office of Senator Charles Danforth of Missouri. Senator Danforth, why are Americans so eager to see James Freeman caned?"

Danforth: "The pro-caning fervor is a reaction to perceived lack of control in the United States over behavior, over emotions. The cause relates to the disintegration of the family, the breakdown of churches as moral forces, the general disintegration of values and norms . . . It's pathetic. People who view caning as somehow the answer are really grasping at straws but a very cruel kind of straw. It's cheap and very offensive and entirely contrary to our values in this country. Discipline within the family is the answer, not caning by the government."

Leong: "Thank you, Senator Danforth. Back to you, Gordon and Jill."

News Anchor Gordon Lau: "We now take you to Duncan Soong, who's at the steps of the U.S. Supreme Court."

Soong: "I am here with Supreme Court Justice Andrew Scarsella. Justice Scarsella, what's your legal opinion about caning?"

Supreme Court Justice Scarsella: "There were worse things than caning in 1791 . . . Caning might even be constitutional now."

Soong: "Back to you, Gordon and Jill."

I never realized how brutal Americans could be. What was happening to my country? Then I remembered what Dad said—that the Singland news may not truly represent opinion in the United States. At least the *New York Times* and the *Philadelphia Inquirer* were on my side. But the Singland government remained adamant as the news broadcast continued:

News Anchor Jill Eng: "Our studio has received a statement from the Press Secretary of the Prime Minister's office in response to the claim that the sentence imposed on James Freeman was excessive. The statement reads as follows":

"There is a misimpression that the American boy merely disfigured two cars with bricks and eggs. Instead, the list of offenses runs much longer. He had initially been charged with a total of 36 counts of vandalism and related offenses. However, after plea bargaining, he was charged with 2 counts of vandalism, 2 counts of mischief, and 1 count of retaining stolen property—all of which he pleaded guilty to.

"In passing sentence on Freeman, the court also took into consideration his admission to 16 counts of vandalism and 5 counts of mischief. Some 14 counts of vandalism and 1 count of possession of dangerous fireworks were withdrawn as a result of the plea bargaining. In the last five years, 12 Singlanders and 2 foreigners have been sentenced to caning for vandalism. In upholding the law, Singland treats both Singlanders and foreigners alike."

Alex then turned the TV channel to a body building contest being held in Jakarta, Indonesia. Mr. Southeast Asia was to be chosen. Once again, I did my duty.

47

Mess Hall

One afternoon the following week, Alex was summoned somewhere, leaving me alone in the cell. When the dinner buzzer rang, I felt hunger pangs. But I was afraid at first to go on my own, thinking he'd return any minute. My hunger won out, so I put on my shorts, walked down the hall and down the steps, and entered the cafeteria. I remembered that I'd been sitting at a table near the food, so I went there and sat down.

The Chinese at the table were there as usual, delighted I was there alone. I looked down, as usual, but they immediately started to make loud sucking sounds. Obviously, they knew I was sucking him.

"Cut it out, guys," I tried to plead, "Do you want Alex to know what you're doing?"

First Chinese Guy (Yen): "We don't care. He might try to beat us, but our bodies are strong enough. Besides, he's not here to defend you, whiteboy."

"He'll be here soon," I bluffed.

Second Chinese Guy (Lim): "He's at a hearing. That'll take some time. Do you know he deliberately *chose* you? Prison management gave him what he wanted."

"He didn't tell me that. But I'm in the cell with him, so it doesn't matter anyway."

"But it matters to us, whiteboy. When he finds a difficult whiteboy to train, he asks all of us to come in and rape the boy. So, while we're waiting for him, whiteboy, stand up and lower your pants. We want to see your lily-white ass! Give us a preview!"

I pretended I didn't hear him.

Soon, when our table was called to get the food, I stood up. A third Chinese prisoner (Chiang) came up to me, lowered my pants, and spanked me, whereupon the rest of the Chinese chimed, "I'm next," laughing heartily.

"Your ass is so pure and white—but not for long," said the fourth guy (Yap).

"Such a small ku ku bird," mocked the fifth guy (Wong). He was referring to my penis.

As I pulled up my pants, Gurkha security guard Bahadur then came over and accused me of deliberately lowering my pants.

"That guy did it," I said, pointing to Chiang.

Just then, Alex came into the room, saw me being questioned, and went to the security guard.

He asked Bahadur, "What's the trouble here?"

"I caught this whiteboy with his pants down," the security guard replied. "He says Chiang did it."

Alex: "I'll handle it now. You can go back to your post."

Bahadur withdrew. I now saw that the prison staff was extremely deferential to Alex.

Alex then criticized Chiang, "You're a toot, a xia suay."

(Toot = stupid person; xia suay = an embarrassment)

We then had lunch together, and I followed him back to our cell.

When we got back in the cell, Alex said,

"I believe you, whiteboy. Chiang is the type who'll engage in stupid pranks. I'll get him at the gym if he dares to show his face. They're all delighted an American has to suffer, but some'll also be caned later, and they won't laugh then."

"Nobody should be caned. It's wrong. Surely my government will stop it, Sir."

"Don't count on it," he said in a harsh tone. He had his own problems with the government. "Despite my fame, the government keeps me in here until Elizabeth gives up on me."

"I'm sorry about that, Sir. Maybe she should go to school in the USA and pretend she's left you. Then they would let you go, Sir."

"That's a good idea, whiteboy. But she has to convince her fucking father to leave the country and abandon his plan to have her married to a boy whose father is high up in the government."

"I wish all the best for you, Sir."

Alex: "Thanks for your support. And thanks for your obedience. You're a good whiteboy!"

As I smiled, he stroked my butt but didn't fuck me that night. We had dinner, showered, and slept until morning. I hoped maybe we were now friends, and that I was no longer his slave. But he continued to insist that I service him, and I still complied.

Alex had rescued me at the mess hall. When he turned on the television five days later, however, I found that someone else wanted to rescue me—President Bill Clinton.

<h1 style="text-align:center">48</h1>

More TV News

News about my caning continued on Singland television almost daily. One broadcast that my Dad saved for me to replay was particularly significant:

News Anchor Jill Eng: "Singland awaits a resolution of questions about the caning of American boy James Freeman. Opinions vary. For another view, we take you to Duncan Soon, our Boston correspondent."

Soong: "I am here with Dr. Frederick Kennedy at the office of the organization Physicians for Human Rights. Dr. Kennedy, some Americans object that caning is too extreme a punishment. What do you think?"

Kennedy: "Physicians for Human Rights is concerned that caning causes bleeding, swelling, and bruising of the buttocks and frequent traumatic shock and scarring. The physical and psychological consequences of this punishment are equivalent to the effects of torture, which is a violation of international covenants. We ask not just for the

193

American boy's sentence to be commuted but also that the punishment be legally abolished. Not just in Singland but worldwide.

"We also seek assurances that current legislation in Singland requiring physician participation during the practice of caning be amended as it contravenes international standards of medical ethics.

"Accordingly, we have addressed a letter on the subject to Singland President Fu Kwang Chu."

Soong: "Thank you, Dr. Kennedy. This is Duncan Soong in Boston. Back to you, Gordon and Jill."

News Anchor Gordon Lau: "We now take you to New York, where our correspondent Sheila Lim is standing by with *New York Times* columnist William Dangerfeld."

Lim: "Mr. Dangerfeld, you have written a column in the *New York Times* about the James Freeman case in Singland. For our Singlander viewers, could you summarize what you said?"

Dangerfeld: "Torture is an act of savagery as old as civilization. In our century, the Nazis delighted in finding new scientific methods for the infliction of pain, while 'tiger cages' were an Asian contribution. Today, caning is not permitted by the International Covenant on Civil and Political Rights, but the government of Singland, along with two other countries, stands aloof from the universal condemnation."

Lim: "What's your opinion of Americans who favor caning and want that form of punishment introduced here in New York?"

Dangerfeld: "Although some Americans espouse torture, they do so thoughtlessly. The only civilized punishments are loss of property (a fine) and/or loss of freedom (a jail sentence). Taking away a convict's freedom punishes but does not inflict pain."

Lim: "What about the death penalty?"

Dangerfeld: "That's not germane. That retributive justice by lethal injection is painless but should be proportionate to the crime."

Lim: "What if Singland won't heed President Bill Clinton's appeal?"

Dangerfeld: "If Singland continues to espouse state-sponsored torture, some 300,000 Americans could stop visiting that country every year or flying its airline. Stockholders and customers of U.S. companies doing business in Singland could re-examine corporate investments and purchases. The use of cheap Singland labor to add value to US exports to Asia could be re-examined.

"Torture is a crime against humanity. How long can Singland prosper as a lawless state?"

Lim: "Thank you, William Dangerfeld. Back to you, Gordon and Jill."

News Anchor Jill Eng: "We now take you to *Sylvia Gomes*, who is standing by with Jonathan Holbron, an American executive who has lived in Singland for six years."

Gomes: "Mr. Holbron, what's your opinion on the James Freeman case?"

Holbron: "Instead of howling in sympathy with the bad guy, American officials should admire the swift, strong arm of Singlish justice. Yes, Freeman's crime has done permanent harm by causing emotional damage—to Singlanders. When he vandalized those cars, he violated his victims' sense of security."

Gomes: "Thank you, Jonathan Holbron. Back to you, Gordon and Jill."

New Anchor Gordon Lau: "We have in our studio, *Straits Times* editorial writer Mohammed Asad. Mr. Asad, what's your opinion on the furor over James Freeman?"

Asad: "Those who editorially oppose Singlish justice chose such intemperate words as dictatorship or lawless state, and even use historical examples of torture in Nazi Germany and ancient Persia that have nothing to do with the present case. Their purpose appears to be to scold those Americans who support the caning, vilify the country which has imposed it, and even threaten Singland with dire consequences.

"What makes the arguments interesting is a single theme. The commentaries assume that Americans do not really understand what the punishment entails.

They go on to claim that caning is no less than torture. They argue that civilized Americans should not support caning, even if they think that their own society has gone soft on crime. The commentaries appear misdirected for several reasons.

"First, it is difficult to accept the proposition that Americans do not know what caning really involves. It is precisely the severity of the punishment that has caused the case to receive widespread publicity.

"Secondly, Americans who support caning and want it introduced in the US do so precisely because it is tough. They consider caning a deterrent to crime.

"Finally, if the objective of the commentators is to ask for compassion for James Freeman, their strategy is very strange. Their sharpened adjectives, chosen to hurt as well as the strident tone, and the generally dismissive style appear to have less to do with a young man awaiting a tough punishment and more with an arrogant indignation over the way the Singland system works."

Lau: "Thank you, Mr. Asad. For a different view, we take you to our correspondent in Washington, Stephen Tam."

Tam: "I am here with James Hoagson at the main offices of the *Washington Post*. Mr. Hoagson, what's your opinion about the sentence imposed on James Freeman?"

Hoagson: "I do not think any person or government has any right to inflict physical pain on another human being. If anything in life is morally wrong, torture is morally wrong. This issue is not about degrees of harshness, nor is it limited to one teenager; it is a case of a state asserting an intolerable 'right to torture.'

"In looking at this problem with Singland, it is not incidental that this country is ruled by ethnic Chinese citizens who have not lost totally the Han emperors' disdain for non-Han cultures.

"This conflict revolves around thousands of years of institutionalized racism practiced by Chinese leaders, from the emperors to the chairman's commissars."

Tam: "This is Stephen Tam with James Hoagson at the *Washington Post*. Back to you, Gordon and Jill."

Until this interview, I hadn't thought about Singland as a racist country, though the term "whiteboy" always bothered me. But I asked my cellmate how that idea squared with the fact that Joey Tan was also being judged by the same laws.

He nodded and then turned to sports. A rugby match was in progress.

49

Second Prison Visit

Support from the American media didn't impress me. What I valued most were the visits from Ling and my family. Well, Ling increasingly became part of my family. My love for her grew throughout my ordeal.

During another prison visit the following week, I felt a lift when they all spoke in soothing terms:

Dad: "Good to see you, son. How have you been?"

"Thanks to my cellmate, Dad, I'm exercising regularly. I'm strengthening my butt and building muscle everywhere else. And I'm getting thinner in my waist with all the lifting."

Ling: "You have the best gym teacher in Singland! You're very lucky, Jim."

"I know. He has been very supportive."

"Ling," I asked, "Have you met Elizabeth Hee, my cellmate's girlfriend?"

Ling: "Yes, we're good friends now. We stand outside the prison at 5 together, looking at your cell. We both hope you'll both come out soon."

"He'll be there indefinitely, I guess, until she leaves the country or something," I speculated.

Ling: "She's talking about going to school in the USA, but she has to save up. Her father won't pay her way."

"When I get out, Ling, maybe my family can help her."

Ling: "I'll tell her that. She'll be very pleased to have more support, as she's very sad."

"So's Alex. He misses her a lot. The way I miss you, Ling."

Ling then blew me a kiss.

Yan, changing the subject: "How's the food?"

"It's Chinese. Plenty of rice every meal. But not kosher. I miss hamburgers, fries, and steaks. And especially your gourmet cooking."

Yan: "When you get out, I'll have a real banquet for you. All your favorite foods."

"Well, don't get into too much trouble." With a big smile, "I can eat only so much at any one meal."

We all laughed.

Dad: "Your Mom in Pennsylvania is trying to get you released by putting pressure on President Clinton and Congress. Your lawyers are preparing a petition to the Singland president to pardon you or at least stop the caning. We're all eager for justice in your case, Jim."

"Thanks, Dad. I appreciate what you're all doing. Too bad the same pressure wasn't applied when our people were being mistreated by the Nazis in the 1930s."

Dad: "Times have changed, Jim. The world has learned a lesson from those dark days. And they are applying that lesson to your case—to get them to stop the caning, not just for you but worldwide."

Agreeing, "I hope so, Dad."

That was all we had time for, so we exchanged kisses through the window, said our goodbyes, and smiled. My love for Ling was stronger than ever.

But some of what Dad said came to pass very soon.

50

More TV News

After the prison visit, I went to my cell. Alex had turned on the television.

News Anchor Gordon Lau: "We take you to a news conference in the White House. The president's Press Secretary, Christopher Podesty, is about to appear to make a statement."

Podesty: "Today, President Bill Clinton wrote a letter to Singland President Fu Kwang Chu. In that letter, he made a personal plea for the government not to cane James Freeman. No more questions."

Podesty then left the room, while reporters shouted questions.

News Anchor Jill Eng: "James Freeman's barristers today handed a 13-page petition for a pardon to a security guard at the palace residence of President Fu Kwang Chu. President Fu has asked the Cabinet to deliberate in response to the petition, and to make a recommendation for him. We have assembled several members of the Cabinet for their comments."

Home Affairs Minister Henry Cheng: "It's absurd that societies so stricken with crime should attempt to apply *their* standards on us and teach *us* what to do . . . They're grabbing at a straw to save James Freeman."

Foreign Minister Krishna Das: "The issue isn't caning but whether one country, the United States, should respect the right of another to enact and enforce its own laws . . . The irony is that the American people are strongly in support of the decision taken by Singland."

Parliamentarian Roger Chua: "Singland people are basically very conservative about crime and punishment. And rightly so. Experience shows that treating criminals with kid gloves doesn't work."

Senior Minister Low Chai Liang: "The clemency petition is much ado about nothing . . . The punishment isn't fatal, though it's not painless. It does what it's supposed to do—remind the wrongdoer that he should never do it again . . . The American should take the medicine like a man."

Eng: "Prime Minister Ho Mang Chin, what will be your recommendation for President Fu Kwang Chu?"

Ho: "The United States is neither safe nor peaceful because it does not dare to restrain or punish those who do wrong. If they like it that way, that's their problem. But that's not the path we Singlanders have chosen.

"Can we govern if we let him off and not cane him? Can we then cane any other foreigner or our own people? We'll have to close shop . . . I'm an old-fashioned man who believes that to govern you must have a certain moral authority. If we do not cane him because he is an American, I believe we'll lose our moral authority and our right to govern."

I then politely asked Alex to change the channel.

He then smiled and turned to sports. We watched an exciting soccer game instead. And I did my evening duty.

51

Third Prison Visit

It was visiting day again the following week. This time, Dad, Yan, Ling, and barrister Suriyakumaran met with me across a glass partition and talked by telephone. Mom had arrived from Philly to join them.

Mom: "Hi, Jim! How are you holding out?"

"Better, now that you're here, Mom."

Mom: "Are you really OK, Jim? You look sleepy?"

Nervous and frightened, I responded,

"Scared of the caning, I've had little sleep."

Dad: "We're proud of you, Jim. Despite everything, you've proved you're better than them."

He gave me a thumbs up, which I reciprocated.

I was about to ask if Ling got the letter that I tried to mail to her, when Ling, with tears running down her cheeks, said:

"I was touched by your letter, Jim. I love you and miss you very much."

"I love you, too, Ling. Your support means, like, a lot to me. All of you."

Dad: "Jim, Are you ready for the caning? Have you hardened your butt with those exercises?"

I assured, "As ready as I can be, Dad. Well, if our people could survive the Holocaust, I can handle a caning. We're survivors."

Mom: "You're right. We *are*, Jim." Turning to the barrister, "When will the president decide whether to grant clemency to Jim?"

Suriyakumaran: "I'm told it'll be soon."

Mom: "If he doesn't stop the caning, I'll demand to see President Clinton. I've organized a petition drive, and we've already collected thousands of signatures."

Dad: "I've been followed by at least 100 Singlish intelligence people over the past months. Your fate is linked to our safety. We will continue to fight for you, Jim."

Upset that I was causing trouble to others, I managed,

"Thanks, Dad."

I next asked, "Ling, have you made good friends with Alex's Elizabeth by now?"

Ling: "Very much so, Jim. She's hopeful that your family might offer to help her move to the USA as a way to free Alex."

Dad: "We're considering that, as you've evidently made good friends with your cellmate."

"I've told him, Ling, and he's excited. As a world-class bodybuilder, his agent might arrange for him to go on tour and end up in the USA to join her."

Ling: "Good plan, Jim."

The visit was cut short by the prison guard. We exchanged goodbyes and good lucks. Mom decided to stay in Singland a few more days. I was *so* happy to have seen her.

Later that day at 5, I saw Ling standing outside, as usual. She was always there, even in the rain, hot sun, or cloudy weather. Like clockwork as well, Alex's girl Elizabeth was also standing outside, hoping for him to come out the door, free at last. And I did my duty to my master.

52

Frustrating TV News

I continued my routine in prison for about two months, getting stronger and stronger, thanks to Alex's help. The guys at the mess table stopped pestering me and instead began to compliment me as I developed some definition in my muscles, including veins that popped out of my inner arms. I guessed they were lusting after me, but Alex held them in check.

Meanwhile, the trial of the Singlander boy, Joey Tan, had been held, and he was sentenced to 12 strokes of the cane. He went to a different prison, however.

The news about me had quieted down. But there were more frustrating developments at the end of that month. Thanks to my cellmate's TV, I heard the following news:

> News Anchor Jill Eng: "James Freeman's mother this morning submitted 700,000 petitions of clemency to overturn her son's caning sentence with President Fu Kwang Chu. She delivered 5 bundles of names from the United States, Australia, Britain, Canada, and Hong Kong to a guard in front of the residence of the Singland President. The names were largely collected

through media appearances on behalf of her son . . . Her petitions were separate from an appeal filed by James Freeman's lawyers yesterday . . . For more on that formal appeal, we now go to our correspondent in Philadelphia, Duncan Soong."

Soong: "I'm at Temple University with Murray Rosen, James Freeman's American attorney. Mr. Rosen was in Singland to represent him and now continues to assist in the litigation."

To Rosen: "An appeal for a pardon was filed with Singland President Fu Kwang Chu yesterday. What's the basis for the appeal?"

Rosen: "We've made a very personal appeal. Our petition says James Freeman is unfit to undergo a caning. Doctors say the fear of the punishment or the punishment itself might drive him to suicide or turn him into an emotional cripple since his neurological illness makes him less able to cope with stress . . . Singland laws allow for such an exception."

Soong: "Are you confident that a pardon will be granted?"

Rosen: "We have to pretty much wait and see what they're going to do."

"This is Duncan Soong at Temple University with James Freeman's American attorney. Back to you, Gordon and Jill."

News Anchor Gordon Lau: "Arnold Choi is standing by the office of James Freeman's father."

Choi: "I'm here at the office of James Freeman's father."

To Dad: "I understand you saw James Freeman in prison last Saturday. What was his mood, now that pressure is mounting for the government to reverse the caning sentence?"

Dad: "James is somber. He reads a lot, and he wanted me to tell others, 'Keep praying for me, I love everyone, and I'm keeping strong inside and outside my body.' They give him only one sheet of paper every week, and he tried to deliver a special message to his girlfriend on Saturday, but the censors took it from him. But he's a realist, and I think he's prepared for any outcome."

Choi: "Back to you, Gordon and Jill."

Eng: "We now take you to the law offices of James Freeman's barristers in Singland. Standing by is our reporter Sylvia Gomes."

Gomes: "Singland Television has heard that you've asked President Fu Kwang Chu for a commutation or a pardon. What's the basis for your request?"

Suriyakumaran: "As a matter of honor, James Freeman refused to testify against Americans Eduardo Ramírez and Bruce Sonnenfeld as well as Oliver Tuanthai of Thailand and Joey Tam of Singland. Accordingly, there was insufficient evidence to convict the Americans and Oliver Tuanthai of Thailand of the most serious crimes, so they paid a fine and escaped caning. Accordingly,

James Freeman should be released from prison or, at a minimum, spared of caning."

Gomes: "What's the reaction of Americans doing business in Singland to the Freeman case?"

Savundranayagam. "Most business executives are concerned that their children might suffer the same fate. They've protested to the government, but quietly . . . The mood seems to be that the butt you save may be your own."

Gomes: "This is Sylvia Gomes with James Freeman's barristers in Singland. Back to you, Gordon and Jill."

Eng: "Thank you, Sylvia. For a view from a Singlander dissident, we take you to our Boston correspondent, Duncan Soong."

Soong: "I'm here at Harvard University with Marshall Seow Liew, a onetime member of an opposition party in Singland who's now living in the United States. Mr. Liew, what are the prospects for James Freeman? Do you think he'll be granted clemency by President Fu Kwang Chu?"

Liew: "It's unfortunate that it takes the caning of a teenage boy to attract the attention of the American president when there is so much repression going on in Singland. Many Singlanders want to abolish caning, but they're shocked that Clinton's concern for human rights seems reserved for a delinquent American teenager, rather than for the others who are caned in Singland each year . . . The government is harping on the obvious double standard, so they have no choice but to cane him."

Soong: "Thank you, Marshall Lieu. This is Duncan Soong at Harvard. Back to you, Gordon and Jill."

News Anchor Gordon Lau: "We now transfer you to our correspondent, Richard Pak, at the office of Prime Minister Ho Mang Chin, who is accompanied by other members of the Cabinet."

Pak: "Prime Minister Ho Mang Chin, what can you tell us about recent developments in the case of James Freeman?"

Ho: "President Fu Kwang Chu has asked the Cabinet for advice on the appeal for clemency for James Freeman, who is petitioning not to be caned for vandalism."

Then other members of the Cabinet spoke up:

Deputy Prime Minister Low: "Interestingly, the Americans are only protesting because we're caning an American. They don't object when our courts sentence Singlanders to be caned. What hypocrisy!"

Home Affairs Minister Cheng: "The main objective is to stop increasing lawlessness among our youth, so I favor caning the American boy."

Information Minister Ong: "It's politically untenable to grant clemency. If we're seen buckling in to media pressure or to political pressure from America, then it's no longer possible for us to govern Singland as an independent country. We become a joke."

Foreign Minister Das: "Our ambassador in Washington indicates that some kind of reprisal might be made if we cane the boy. Americans could boycott Singlish goods."

Home Affairs Minister Cheng: "Not a chance. There are too many American businesses here. It would hurt them bad."

Senior Minister Low: "We've banned American publications by restricting their circulation down to almost nothing, and they've never banded together because it's in their interest to stay here. Businesses like the fact that we stifle strikes and any form of political opposition to maintain stability . . . As for human rights, the American people want the caning. They have a lot of crime and wish they could cane their criminals."

Cheng: "The Western cliché that it would be better for a guilty person to go free than to convict an innocent person is testimony to the importance of the individual. But an Asian perspective may well be that it is better that an innocent person be convicted if the common welfare is protected than for a guilty person to be free to inflict further harm on the community."

Deputy Prime Minister Low: "What about the sentence of the Singlander boy, Joey Tan, who's also pleading for clemency from President Fu for a sentence of 12 strokes of the cane? Do Americans object when a Singlander boy is to be caned?"

Ho: "Excellent point. The parents of Joey Tan are much more humbly and quietly pleading for clemency, but we can't cane one without the other. All over the world, everyone should see we're fair, while Americans are just playing superpower bully and don't really care about human rights."

Members of the Cabinet nodded and smiled approvingly to one another.

Pak: "Back to you, Gordon and Jill."

Lau: "Thank you, Richard Pak . . . That's the news for today. Stay tuned for more late-breaking developments on the James Freeman case."

Alex then turned to sports, including the one he enjoyed with me.

53

Clemency Denied

Then came the decision on whether to cane me, as announced on evening television, after dinner, and before my shower for the night.

News Anchor Jill Eng: "This evening, President Fu Kwang Chu today is to release his long-awaited decision on American James Freeman's appeal for clemency to cancel his caning sentence. Our cameras are now at the presidential palace, where he is about to announce his decision:"

Fu: "President Bill Clinton and others have asked me to reconsider the decision of our courts to cane American teenager James Freeman, who was convicted of vandalism earlier this year.

"I therefore consulted the Prime Minister and his Cabinet for a recommendation. They deliberated at length, and I have considered their response over the past weeks with a view to rendering justice in this case.

"On the merits of the case, I didn't find any grounds for commuting James Freeman's caning sentence, and I can't compromise the principle that persons convicted of vandalism must be caned.

"As for the alleged mitigating factors, Freeman is an adult, and his case must be handled like any other— without favoritism. Only children and older persons are exempt from caning. Moreover, the evidence contradicts allegations of police torture to extract his confession.

"However, to reject Mr. Clinton's appeal outright would show an unhelpful disregard for the President of the United States and for the domestic pressures on him on this issue. The government values good relations with the United States and the constructive economic and security role of the United States in the region.

"Accordingly, as a goodwill gesture to President Clinton, I've ordered that the number of strokes of the cane shall be reduced from 6 to 4."

I was mortified that I really would be caned, but at least I would suffer less. My cellmate Alex had been stepping up my butt exercises, and they were getting much firmer. I hoped to have a hard body like him, but that might take years. I was prepared to accept my fate as an obedient man. Alex had trained me to enjoy obeying.

54

More Bad TV News

Early that morning, after I showered but before breakfast, Alex turned on the TV to learn the reaction to the Singland president's announcement.

News Anchor Jill Eng: "President Fu Kwang Chu yesterday reduced the sentence of James Freeman, an American teenager convicted of vandalizing cars, to receive 4 strokes of the cane instead of the 6 ordered by the courts. Here's an official comment from Home Affairs Minister Shiu-Feng Cheng:"

Cheng: "The government fully supports President Fu Kwang Chu's decision . . . Regarding allegations of police torture, an internal police investigation of the treatment of Freeman revealed that the complaint has no basis. Freeman's conviction was based on his guilty plea in open court and not on the statement of confession that he gave to the police . . . Officials have caned 450 people for vandalism in the past year, and all but 2 were Singlanders. To say he's being singled out is absurd."

News Anchor Gordon Lau: "We also asked Samuel Walker, an American business executive from New York who works here in Singland, what he thinks about the sentence. Here's what he said to our reporter Sylvia Gomes."

Walker: "James, at 18, is old enough to know the penalties. We're guests here and when you're in Rome, you do as the Romans do."

Eng: "Now, for the American reaction, here's a news conference earlier today in Washington."

Journalist David Donaldson: "President Clinton today responded to increasing pressure to make a statement about Singland's decision to cane 18-year-old James Freeman."

Clinton: "The United States has made a strong protest to Singland for the decision to cane James Freeman of Newton Square, Philadelphia. This punishment is extreme, and we hope very much that it will be reconsidered."

News Anchor Gordon Lau: "We now go live to Arthur Gilbert of Philadelphia television station WDAY, who's on Main Street in Newton Square, Pennsylvania, for a sampling of public opinion in James Freemans's hometown."

I could see pedestrians walking along the only downtown street. A camera was put in front of several persons, who gave their opinions.

Rod Murtaugh: "I have no sympathy for young Mr. Freeman. How often in this country do we see criminals in fear? Interesting how troublemakers don't like a dose of their own medicine. Damage property here and you don't get punished, but the property owner is stuck with the bill."

Chris Waife: "I'll bet you dollars to doughnuts this guy never does it again. We should do it in this country. Five or six whacks on the can with a cat-o'-nine-tails is a great deterrent."

Jennie Adams: "I feel sorry for the lad. They shouldn't use a cane. That's barbaric."

Claude Hill: "He chose to disobey the law, knowing the consequence. We were recently in Singland and found the city head and shoulders above any others in cleanliness. Caning should make anyone think twice before being lawless."

Lloyd Lavin: "That American punk is getting exactly what he deserves. If we had similar laws, I'm sure the streets of Philadelphia wouldn't be under control of the thugs and slugs."

Tim Thornblad: "I have no problem with the sentence. Clinton should keep his red nose out of Singland's business."

Leah Triska: "I wish something like that could be done here with these punks and their graffiti. I have no sympathy. I don't. I don't!"

Dick Chenoweth: "We should go to the dark side with some criminals and let them know the price that they'll pay."

News Reporter Gilbert: "That's how the public here feels. This is Arthur Gilbert, from Main Street in downtown Newton Square, Pennsylvania. Back to you, Gordon and Jill."

News Anchor Jill Eng: "We now turn to our reporter Malcolm Ing, who is with Murray Rosen, the American lawyer who tried to negotiate James Freeman's release."

Ing: "Mr. Rosen, what do you think about public opinion in America regarding the decision to cane James Freeman?"

Rosen: "In my opinion, by running so many stories in favor of caning, without explaining that James Freeman confessed to vandalism because of police torture and that Singland welched on his plea bargain, the media's contributing to the hysteria that enabled Singland to cane him."

Ing: "It's the same all across the country at all the TV stations. Viewer ratings have shot up through the roof since American television stations started carrying the story. Advertisers are clamoring to run spots on news shows now."

Rosen: "I suppose you're right. I've seen a lot of new ads for Preparation H."

They both grimaced.

Ing: "This is Malcolm Ing in Philadelphia. Back to you, Gordon and Jill."

News Anchor Lau: "For a comment from Prime Minister Ho Mang Chin, we now go to our reporter Sylvia Gomes at his residence."

Gomes: "Prime Minister Ho Mang Chin, what's your opinion about the decision to go ahead with the caning of James Freeman as well as the strong interest of public opinion in this case?"

Ho: "The President of Singland has made his decision. In my opinion, case closed. I have nothing more to say."

Gomes: "The prime minister has spoken few words. But the words have considerable weight in calming the uproar for the people of Singland. Back to you, Gordon and Jill."

Eng: "In other news today, 4 foreigners found guilty of drug possession were hanged today after appeals for clemency to President Fu Kwang Chu were rejected. Since the death penalty was imposed for drug possession in 1975, some 52 people drug dealers have been hanged in Singland . . ."

I was very disheartened by the news. The public evidently wanted me caned. I had to prepare for the worst.

Soon after the news announcement that the sentence had been reduced to 4 strokes of the cane, my barrister Savundranayagan went alone to see me in prison. A guard summoned me to the visiting area. After delivering the news, I told him to thank my family and asked them to pray for me. I also asked him to thank President Clinton and President Fu for their intervention. I wondered when the caning would take place, and he told me that usually caning is carried out quickly after all legal channels have been exhausted.

Alex then turned off the TV and snapped his finger so he could use one of my channels. Another butt exercise to prepare me.

55

The Caning

When my barrister left, I went back to my cell. A Gurkha guard appeared soon in a black uniform. He entered my cell, asked me to put on my shorts, and then escorted me to the room where the caning was to take place. It was almost three months since I was imprisoned.

Upon entering the room, I saw a trestle peaking at 4 feet in height and slanting down on both sides. A Prison Official greeted me. The Caner, a muscular kung-fu master wearing only a black jockstrap, was standing by with a 4-foot-long ½-inch-wide rattan cane in a container of water. (Alex later told me that the instrument was soaked overnight in a brine solution to prevent splinters from residing in the butt, while the salt served an antiseptic purpose.) The Caner was almost as muscular as Alex. His body looked greased, and he wasn't masked. In fact, he was rather handsome. A prison physician, wearing a white uniform and gloves, was seated at a table with a few medical instruments and ointments. The room was very cold.

Prison Official, pointing to a chair next to the trestle:

"Strip off."

I removed my pants and placed them on the chair.

The Prison Physician came up to me, took my blood pressure and pulse, nodded to the Prison Official, then made a sign to a Prison Guard, who next shackled my hands and ankles with leather wrist straps, spreadeagled to the A-shaped wood trestle with my butt exposed. The Prison Guard then placed small pillows under my head and navel. My genitals were covered and taped to the front of my body. Protective rubber cushions were placed over the kidney area and below my butt, presumably to prevent damage to internal organs and the spine. A mouth gag was fitted, I guess to prevent tongue biting and to muffle screams. I sensed that the prison physician then nodded to the Prison Official.

> Prison Official: "James Alan Freeman, you have been
> sentenced to 4 strokes of the cane. Sentence will now
> be carried out."

I was perspiring and fearful.

> Prison Official: "Count one!"

After removing the rattan cane from the container of water, the Caner dried the cane and held the instrument rigidly at arm's length. He walked forward 3 steps, pivoted on his feet, and delivered the first stroke with all his might. A sharp crack, like a rifle shot, echoed.

Trying to scream and struggle like an animal, I felt a deep boring sensation throughout my body. Real pain. It burned all through my body. I felt soreness from skin in my butt being split. All that exercise didn't give me immunity from pain. I tried to yell "I'm dying" but the words did not come out.

> Prison official, soothingly: "OK, James. Three left."

The Caner then put the cane back in the bucket.

The prison physician then inspected the reddish skin, which was split open and put an antiseptic ointment on the broken blood vessels. After taking my blood pressure, he nodded OK to the prison official.

Prison official: "Count two!"

The Caner took the cane out of the bucket, dried it with a cloth, took up his position, and administered the second stroke.

I felt a shiver down my back. I thought that I would have scars for the rest of my life.

Prison official, more routinely: "OK, James. Two left."

The Caner put the instrument back into the water.

The prison physician inspected the two wounds, which were now bleeding and swollen, placed ointment on the wounds, took my blood pressure, and then nodded OK to the prison official.

Prison official: "Count three!"

The Caner administered the third stroke after the same procedure.

Pieces of skin were visibly flying past me. I tried to say "Owww!" Then I urinated. Into my mind was an intense hatred for the government. I promised myself that I was going to do something about this government when I got out. They would have to pay a price!

The prison guard, evidently somewhat shaken by the blood that he saw dripping down to the floor:

"OK, James. One more. You're almost done."

The prison physician inspected the three wounds, which were dribbling blood because pieces of skin were severed. He placed ointment on the wounds, took my blood pressure, and then nodded OK to the Prison Official.

Prison official: "Count four!"

The cane came out of the container. The Caner wiped the rattan instrument dry, took position, and applied the final stroke. It was all over.

The prison physician inspected the wounds, which were dripping more blood than before, placed more ointment on the wounds, took my blood pressure, and then nodded OK to the prison official, who in turn nodded to the Prison Guard.

The prison guard then removed all the padding from my body and unshackled me from the trestle. When the mouth guard was removed, I made a loud scream.

With my face contorted, I tried to stand up. I extended my hand to the Caner, and we shook hands. I wanted to show I'd kept my pride—that I could take it like a man. I didn't ever want to lose my pride. He was only doing his job in this goddamn police state.

But immediately after shaking hands, my knees buckled, and I fell to the floor. The prison guard caught me and propped me up. The prison physician then got a stretcher down from the wall. The Prison Guard eased me, staggering, onto the stretcher face down. Another prison guard was summoned while I rested on the stretcher.

Then the two prison guards carried me naked out of the room to the prison hospital ward. My butt was quite bloodied. A Prison Nurse put an intravenous needle in my left arm, turned me on one side, and I muttered cries of pain. I guess they gave me something to make me sleep while feeding me intravenously in the prison hospital.

Five hours later, when I began to wake up, my body was still shaking with pain. My butt had swollen up. My thighs went blue-black, and my legs didn't work at first because the caning evidently had an effect on my hamstring muscles.

(Thanks to the Internet, anyone reading these words can go online and see a caning of a prisoner, Singland style.)

Later, I learned that I was one of 10 persons caned that day.

<h1 style="text-align:center">56</h1>

After the Caning

In the morning, the hospital crew helped me to get up. I stood a minute, and next tried to sit on the bed. Then I stood again and tried to walk, but soon returned to lie down on the bed. They exchanged the intravenous fluid, and I stayed in the prison hospital for most of the rest of the day, sleeping and resting.

A television set in the hospital room had the morning news:

> News Anchor Jill Eng: "Yesterday, Singland caned American teenager James Freeman. As a goodwill gesture to President Clinton, President Fu Kwang Chu had reduced the number of strokes from 6 to 4. Here's what President Clinton had to say about the caning:"

> Clinton: "I think it was a mistake, as I said before, not only because of the nature of the punishment related to the crime but because of the questions that were raised about whether the young man was in fact guilty and involuntarily confessed."

News Anchor Gordon Lau: "For the reaction of a Singlander dissident who now is a scholar at Harvard University, we now take you to our correspondent in Boston, Duncan Soong."

Duncan Soong: "I'm here with Marshall Seow at Harvard University. Mr. Seow, was the caning of James Freeman inevitable?"

Seow: "Anyone in Singland can be detained without trial or even a formal charge and can be tortured without due process of law . . . As soon as James Freeman was reportedly tortured in jail, it was obvious what would come next . . . There was no hope after senior ministers kept up a steady drumbeat of statements defending the use of the cane on him, with official press releases and selected readers' letters supporting the caning in government-controlled newspapers."

Soong: "The Singland government believes that caning Freeman and the death penalty for various offenses will deter crime. What do you think?"

Seow: "I see every year an increase in the number of canings and death sentences imposed, which suggests that these extreme punishments are not acting as a deterrent."

Soong: "Thank you, Marshall Seow. This is Duncan Soong at Harvard. Back to you, Gordon and Jill."

Eng: "For a reaction in Singland, we turn to Sylvia Gomes, who is with Professor Sang Peng Woon, a nominated member of parliament, at Singland University."

Gomes: "Professor Sang, some American leaders don't accept the caning of James Freeman as a routine event. Why is that?"

Professor Sang: "In Britain and in America, they keep very strongly to the presumption of innocence. The prosecution must prove that you are guilty. And even if the judge may feel that you are guilty, he cannot convict you unless the prosecution has proven it. So, in some cases, it becomes a game between the defense and the prosecuting counsel. We Singlanders would rather convict even if it doesn't accord with the purist's traditions of the presumption of innocence. Toughness is considered a virtue here. The system is stacked against criminals. The theory is that a person shouldn't get off on fancy arguments."

Gomes: "We understand that last year, you and your family were robbed at gunpoint at a bus stop near Disneyworld in Orlando, Florida. What's your opinion of the American legal system as a result?"

Sang: "America's legal system has gone completely berserk. They're so mesmerized by the rights of the individual that they forget that victims have rights, too. There's all this focus on the perpetrator and his rights, and they forget the fellow is a criminal. James Freeman is no more than that. His mother and father have no sense of shame. Do they not feel any shame for not having brought him up properly to respect other people's property? Instead, they consider themselves victims."

Gomes: "What about the punishment—the caning? Do you believe that the American boy was punished too much?"

Sang: "No matter how harsh your punishments, you're not going to get an orderly society unless the culture is in favor of order. In Britain and America, they seem to have lost the feeling that people are responsible for their own behavior. Here, there's still a sense of personal responsibility. If you do something against the law, you bring shame not only to yourself but to your family. That sense of shame is more powerful than draconian laws. Loosening up won't mean there will be chaos. But the law must be seen to work. The punishment is not the main thing. It's the enforcement of the law. The law has to be enforced effectively and fairly. If you have friends in high places, that means you get a reduction. One law for Americans and one law for other people is totally unsatisfactory."

Gomes: "Why didn't Americans and Singlanders agree on matters of the law in the case of James Freeman?"

Sang: "The affair was purely and simply an argument about crime and punishment that could and is taking place within America itself. It's not so much a clash of civilizations, as a clash between a conservative society willing to punish when punishment is called for and a liberal society where people—or at least the liberal establishment—are apologetic about punishing criminals. Within the United States, there will be conservative groups who share with us the same beliefs in hard work, thrift, personal responsibility, and the value of the family. It's the old Protestant work ethic. It just doesn't seem to percolate upwards in America."

Gomes: "Thank you for your thoughts, Professor Sang Peng Woon. Back to you, Gordon and Jill."

News Anchor Gordon Lau: "That's all the news for this morning. Be sure to stay tuned to the evening news at 6."

Theme song, etc.

At midnight, when all was quiet, a Gurkha escorted me back to my cell, where Alex was fast asleep. He never bothered me after that. From the time I returned to my cell, I slept on my side in the bunk bed, and he was a source of support for me.

For the first five days, it was very hard to sit, and I felt a lot of pain. After that, my butt itched a lot. I couldn't sleep on my back . . . At first, they wouldn't let me shower, telling me that I might get permanent sores.

When I did finally shower, they let me do so alone to avoid injury from other inmates . . . From then on, I tried not to think about the pain. I thought my butt would never look normal again. With my fingers, I felt the scars and the skin drooping.

As I was told later, caning left me with three dark-brown scars on my right butt and four lines, each about half-an-inch wide, on my left butt. Although the wounds healed before I left prison, I have never looked at them.

57

Prison Visit After the Caning

Dad, Yan, and Ling came to visit me in the prison, but I couldn't sit down. I was happy to see them and almost forgot about my pain during our 15 minutes together, as we looked at each other and talked by telephone.

Dad: "You'll be getting out in about 6 weeks, Jim, and we'll have a celebration for you then."

"No, Dad," I said somewhat humbly, "I just want to be free. That will be enough joy for me."

Yan: "We'll make you feel at home again, Jim."

"Singland isn't my home, Yan. It never was. It never will be. When I get out, I want to go back to the USA."

To Dad: "Tell Mom in Pennsylvania that I never thought it would turn out so bad."

Ling: "But you know I love you, Jim."

Realizing that I might be hurting her feelings, I said,

"I love you, too, Ling. Let's go to America together. We can live with my mother and go to college in Philadelphia."

Ling: "I like that idea, Jim. We've got to think about the future. I love you *so* much."

"I love you, too, Ling," I said passionately.

As the guard escorted them out, we exchanged kiss signs. Her faithfulness was a promise of a brand-new life. We waved at each other as they went out the visiting door.

They came again every Saturday—May 14, 21, 28, and June 4, 11, and 18. Saturdays were the best days of the week while in Queenstown Remand Prison.

58

My Release

In the early morning, six weeks after my caning, I was summoned to the main office of the prison and informed that I was to be released for "good behavior" within 24 hours, I was ordered to leave the country. In other words, I was being deported. I was told that my passport was at the departure checkpoint at the airport.

At 9 a.m., Mom (who had recently come from Pennsylvania), Dad, Yan, Ling, and the two lawyers were waiting with 20 journalists outside the prison gate. As I walked out of prison, with some effort to avoid pain, cameras flashed.

> Hugging and kissing me, Mom said, "You're free, Jim. We all love you."

> Dad hugged me and said, "I'm proud of you, Jim."

> Ling, hugging and kissing me, congratulated, "It's finally over, Jim. I missed you a lot, lah. I'll always treasure the letters you wrote me from prison."

Kissing her,

"It's *so* good to see you all at last. But I can't stay another day here in Torture City. I have 24 hours to vamoose."

Mom: "I've reserved for us seats on a flight home tonight, Jim, so you'll be out of this hell hole very soon."

News Anchor Jill Eng, putting a microphone in front of me, "James Freeman, what do you have to say after 122 days in prison?"

"I'm happy to be out. My health is good. I'm looking forward to the future very much. I'm going back to my own country. I just want to get back to the United States and lead a normal life . . . No more questions."

Dad, Mom, Yan, Ling, and I then got inside an awaiting limousine. We went up to Dad's penthouse, and I began to pack my things. Ling joined me in my room and broke down, telling me that she, too, had suffered during the ordeal. We embraced as never before, and I used a tissue to dry her eyes. She then went out, and Ling hugged her.

After packing, I took a shower, put on my Philadelphia shirt and jeans, and went out to the living room.

Yan had fixed some of my favorite foods for a delicious lunch, and we had a sort of banquet together.

Sitting on a soft pillow, I asked,

"Could I take this on the plane?"

Dad: "Sure, Jim. They won't mind. Take two or three if you like."

> Mom: "We're flying first class, Jim. Everything will
> be comfortable. Bring 'em along!"

First class! I was truly grateful for such wonderful support. Fortunately, nobody brought up the subject of my butt, and nobody asked me about my strange prison life.

After the meal, we all left for the airport. Dad, Yan, and Ling accompanied us as far as they could go to the security checkpoint. Dad and Yan hugged me, and I kissed Ling, who had tears in her eyes. We said farewell. I told Ling that I hoped she could join me soon.

> She said, "As soon as I can, Jim. Our love will *never*
> die."

As I went through the passport checkpoint, the official glared at me. Then I walked alongside Mom down past duty-free shops to the departure gate.

As the door opened to my airplane, I joined Mom in boarding an airplane and going to the first-class cabin, pillow in hand for my butt.

While the plane was in the air, the sun began to set. Many hours later, I was back in Newton Square, Pennsylvania, unpacking my things in my room. The ordeal had come to an end.

But the memory still lingers . . .

59

Epilogue

Even though I'm scarred for life, I try not to think about the experience. But I still have nightmares of the arrest, sex with Alex, many humiliations, and the caning. . . In my opinion, the Singland government wasn't completely responsible. Even though I was a victim of injustice, Americans who wanted Singland to cane me for something I didn't do are also responsible.

Two weeks after my caning, I read that Joey Tan had been caned. Not 4 strokes of the cane but 12! The Singland government was sending yet another signal to the youth of the country.

But Joey and I were mere pawns in the calculations of brutal government leaders. And my lower sentence than Joey proved that justice depends upon whether you have friends in high places, something clearly intended to make ordinary Singlanders fear their government—though for many, the correct verb would be "despise" more than "fear."

When I returned to the good old USA, I tried to maintain a low profile, but news reporters kept hounding me for interviews for days. Mom finally suggested that I should do one and tell all the others that I had nothing more to say. Maybe they then would stop bothering me. So I was interviewed for 15 minutes on *Larry King Live*. I said that I did pick up road signs, didn't use spraypaint, confessed because I was tortured, did not enjoy prison life, and that the scars on my body would be with me for life. I suggested that American businesses should pull out of Singland. That was all.

Later that year, I heard that a couple of books were written about my experience, though I wasn't interviewed for them. The authors were Singlanders. One patted the government on its un-caned backside. The other one was written by a critic of the government. I have read neither book. I decided then to stop thinking about my time in Torture City. Instead, I focused on my life in the City of Brotherly Love.

I stayed home instead of finishing my senior year of high school. Nevertheless, I applied for admission to Temple University in Philadelphia, and I was accepted.

When the school year in Singland ended, Ling came to the USA. She had also applied and been accepted at Temple University. After four years, we graduated, married, and went to law school at the University of Pennsylvania. We became Philadelphia lawyers, the envy of the nation!

Alex's girlfriend joined us at Temple University. Alex flew out two months afterward to join her. He established a martial arts school in Philly. They married, and we see them a lot. We've never talked about the secret time when we were cellmates, and he no longer calls me "whiteboy."

Dad relocated his business from Singland to Japan. No other business moved out in protest. President Clinton evidently snubbed Singland officials until he left office. Several newspapers editorially urged the United States to resist Singland's proposal to host the first ministerial meeting of the World Trade Organization in 1996. U.S. Trade Representative Mickey Cantor agreed at first to go elsewhere, but the meeting was ultimately held as scheduled—over my disfigured butt.

Yet nowadays, in the twenty-first century, about 1,200 persons are still caned each year in Singland. As recently as 2018, new offenses were included on the list of about forty crimes for which caning could be applied as punishment. All the claims about deterrence were propaganda, to satisfy the lust of the leaders of the country for sexualizing punishment by applying a cane to a butt. Making me an example to Singlanders didn't deter crime in that rogue totalitarian regime, where opposition candidates are routinely sued and bankrupted after elections to stifle dissent.

I want the world to know what I experienced through the words that I have now written, and I feel much better for letting it all out, uncensored.

The debate in the United States over my caning has taken on a new significance today. Despite international criticism, Singland had long gotten away with torture-produced confessions and severe punishment for what they called "terrorism." In effect, they won the debate about caning by providing a model for dealing with a serious crime.

Americans who wanted me caned, thus accepting the Singland example, later applied that model to deal with persons accused of terrorism. After 9/11, American counterterrorism policy became Singlandized at Bagram Air Force Base in Afghanistan, the American Naval Base in Guantánamo, Cuba, and Abu Ghraib, a prison in Iraq.

It is well known that the American government deliberately inflicted torture inside secret prisons within various countries and at the prison in Guantánamo. And no person has been held accountable under

American law for the use of torture sanctioned by the government in Washington. The United States fell in line with the government of Singland.

Is there a link between Americans who approved my torture and those today who have supported or remained silent about the use of torture by the US government?

What happened after my caning was an upsurge in mandatory sentencing laws: During the 1994 election, which was contested mostly after my caning, the Republican Party accused Democrats of being "soft on crime" and won in a landslide. The same philosophy of throwing the book at anyone *accused* of terrorism still prevails, though torture is no longer used. Now the problem is domestic terrorism.

Today, nevertheless, I have a bright future ahead. My wife and I now live and work in a Philadelphia law office as attorneys for international clients. We have two beautiful biracial children who are now graduating from high school—one boy, one girl. Soon, they will be off to college.

I changed my name in law school to avoid the paparazzi throughout my life, and they've never been told about my brief stay in Singland. The press now tells me that they're proud of me for my work on behalf of human rights.

So, I now write my confession pseudonymously. Historians may say someday that the turn toward the politics of cruelty within the age of impunity began with my case.

But that's another story . . .